THE
AUTOBIOGRAPHY
OF A FLEA

THE
AUTOBIOGRAPHY
OF A FLEA

BY ANONYMOUS

CARROLL & GRAF PUBLISHERS, INC.
New York

Carroll & Graf Publishers, Inc.
260 Fifth Avenue
New York, NY 10001

ISBN: 0-88184-002-5

Printed in the United States of America

THE
AUTOBIOGRAPHY
OF A FLEA

CHAPTER I

Born I was—but how, when, or where I cannot say; so I must leave the reader to accept the assertion ''per se,'' and believe it if he will. One thing is equally certain, the fact of my birth is not one atom less veracious than the reality of these memoirs, and if the intelligent student of these pages wonders how it came to pass that one in my walk—or perhaps, I should have said jump—in life, became possessed of the learning, observation and power of committing to memory the whole of the wonderful facts and disclosures I am about to relate. I can only remind him that there are intelligences, little suspected by the vulgar, and laws in nature, the very existence of which have not yet been detected by the advanced among the scientific world.

I have heard it somewhere remarked that my province was to get my living by blood sucking. I am not the lowest by any means of that universal fraternity, and if I sustain a precarious existence upon the bodies of those with whom I come in contact, my own experience proves that I do so in a marked and peculiar manner, with a warning of my employment which is seldom given by those in other grades of my profession. But I submit that I have other and nobler aims than the mere sustaining of my being by the contributions of the unwary. I have been conscious of this original defect, and, with a soul far above the vulgar instincts of my race. I jumped by degrees to heights of mental perception and erudition which placed me for ever upon a pinnacle of insect-grandeur.

It is this attainment to learning which I shall evoke in describing the scenes of which I have been a witness— nay, even a partaker. I shall not stop to explain by what means I am pessessed of human powers of thinking and observing, but, in my lucubrations, leave you simply to perceive that I possess them and wonder accordingly.

You will thus perceive that I am not common flea; indeed, when it is born in mind the company in which I have been accustomed to mingle, the familiarity with which I have been suffered to treat persons the most exalted, and the opportunities I have possessed to make the most of my acquaintances, the reader will no doubt agree with me that I am in very truth a most wonderful and exalted insect.

My earliest recollections lead me back to a period when I found myself within a church. There was a rolling of rich music and a slow monotonous chanting which then filled me with surprise and admiration, but I have long since learnt the true important of such influences, and the attitudes of the worshippers are now taken by me for the outward semblance of inward emotions which are very generaly non-existent. Be this as it may, I was engaged upon professional business connected with the plump white leg of a young lady of some fourteen years of age, the taste of whose delicious blood I well remember, and the flavour of whose—

But I am digressing.

Soon after commencing in a quiet and friendly way my little attentions, the young girl in common with the rest of the congregation rose to depart, and I, as a matter of course, determined to accompany her.

I am very sharp of sight as well as of hearing, and that is, how I saw a young gentleman slip a small folded piece of white paper into the young lady's pretty gloved hand, as she passed through the crowded porch. I had noticed the name Bella neatly worked upon the soft silk stocking which had at first attracted me, and I now saw that the same word appeared alone upon the outside of the billet-doux. She was with her Aunt, a tall, stately dame, with whom I did not care to get upon terms of intimacy.

Bella was a beauty—just fourteen—a perfect figure, and although so young, her soft bosom was already budding into those proportions which delight the other sex. Her face was charming in its frankness; her breath sweet as the perfumes of Arabia, and, as I have always said, her skin as soft as velvet. Bella was evidently well aware of her good looks, and carried her head as proudly and as coquettishly

9

as a queen. That she inspired admiration was not difficult to see by the wistful and longing glances which the young men, and sometimes also those of the more nature years, cast upon her. There was a general hush of conversation outside the building, and a turning of glances generally towards the pretty Bella, which told more plainly than words that she was the admired one of all eyes and the desired one of all hearts—at any rate among the male sex.

Paying, however very little attention to what was evidently a matter of every-day occurence, the young lady walked sharply homewards with her Aunt, and after arrival at the neat and genteel residence, weat quickly to her room. I will not say I followed, but I "went with her," and beheld the gentle girl raise one dainty leg across the other and remove the tiniest of tight and elegant kid-boots.

I jumped upon the carpet and proceeded with my examinations. The left boot followed, and without removing her plump calf from off the other, Bella sat looking at the folded piece of paper which I had seen the young fellow deposit secretly in her hand.

Closely watching everything. I noted the swelling thighs, which spread upwards above her tightly fitting garters, until they were lost in the darkness, as they closed together at a point where her beautiful belly met them in her stooping position; and almost obliterated a thin and peach-like slit, which just shewed its rounded lips between them in the shade.

Presently Bella dropped her note, and being open, I took the liberty to read it.

"I will be in the old spot at eight o'clock to night," were the only words which the paper contained, but they appeared to have a special interest for Bella, who remained cogitating for some time in the same thoughtful mood.

My curiosity had been aroused, and my desire to know more of the interesting young being with whom chance had so promiscuously brought me in pleasing contact, prompted me to remain quietly ensconced in a snug though somewhat moist hiding place, and it was not until near upon the hour named that I once more emerged in order to watch the progress of events.

Bella had dressed herself with scrupuleus care, and now prepared to betake herself to the garden which surrounded the country-house in which she dwelt.

I went with her.

Arriving at the end of a long and shady avenue the young girl seated herself upon a rustic bench, and there awaited the coming of the person she was to meet.

It was not many minutes before the young man presented himself whom I had seen in communication with my fair little friend in the morning.

A conversation ensued which, if I might judge by the abstraction of the pair from aught besides themselves, had unusual interest for both.

It was evening, and the twilight had already commenced: the air was warm and genial, and the young pair sat closely entwined upon the bench, lost to all but their own united happiness.

"You don't know how I love you Bella," whispered the youth., tenderly sealing his protestation with a kiss upon the pouting lips of his companion.

"Yes I do," replied the girl, naively, "are you not always telling me? I shall get tired of hearing it soon."

Bella fidgetted her pretty little foot and looked thoughtful.

"When are you going to explain and show me all those funny things you told me about?" asked she, giving a guick glance up, and then as rapidly bending her eyes upon the gravel walk.

"Now," answered the youth. "Now, dear Bella, while we have the chance to be alone and free from interruption. You know, Bella, we are no longer children?"

Bella nodded her head.

"Well, there are things which are not known to children, and which are necessary for lovers not only to know, but also to practice."

"Dear me," said the girl, seriously.

"Yes," continued her companion, "there are secrets which render lovers happy, and which make the enjoy of loving and of being loved."

"Lord!" exclaimed Bella, "how, sentimental you have grown, Charlie; I remember the time when you declared sentiment was "all humbug."

"So I thought it was, till I loved you," replied the youth.

"Nonsense," continued Bella, "but go on, Charlie, and tell me what you promised."

"I can't tell you without shoving you as well," replied Charlie; "the knowledge can only be learnt by experience."

"Oh, go on then and show me," caried the girl, in whose bright eyes and glowing cheeks I thought I could detect a very conscious knowledge of the kind of instruction about to be imparted.

There was something catching in her impatience. The youth yielded to it, and covering her beautiful young form with his own, glued his mouth to hers and kissed it rapturously.

Bella made no resistance; she even aided and returned her lover's caresses.

Meanwhile the evening advanced: the trees lay in the

gathering darkness, spreading their lofty tops to screen the waning light from the young lovers.

Presently Charlie slid on one side; he made a slight movement, and then without any epposition he passed his hand under and up the petticoats of the pretty Bella. Not satisfied with the charms which he found within the compass of the glistening silk stockings, he essayed to press on still further, and his wandering fingers now touched the soft and quivering flesh of her young thighs.

Bella's breath came hard and fast, as she felt the indelicate attack which was being made upon her charms. So far, however, from resisting, she evidently enjoyed the exciting dalliance.

"Touch it," whispered Bella, "you may."

Charlie needed no further invitation: indeed he was already preparing to advance without one and instantly comprehending the permission, drove his fingers forward.

The fair girl opened her thighs as he did so, and the next instant his hand covered the delicate pink lips of her pretty slit.

For the next ten minutes the pair remained almost motionless, their lips joined and their breathing alone marking the sensations which were overpowering them with the intoxication of wantoness. Charlie felt a delicate object, which stiffened beneath his nimble fingers, and assumed a prominence of which he had no experience.

Presently Bella closed her eyes, and throwing back her head, shuddered slightly, while her frame became supple and languid, and she suffered her head to rest upon the arm of her lover.

"Oh, Charlie," she murmured, "what is it you do? What delightful sensations you give me."

Meanwhile the youth was not idle, but having fairly

explored all he could in the constrained position in which he found himself, he rose, and sensible of the need of assuaging the raging passion which his actions had fanned, he besought his fair companion to let him guide her hand to a dear object, which he assured her was capable of giving her far greater pleasure that his fingers had done.

Nothing loth, Bella's grasp was the next moment upon a new and delicious substance, and either giving way to the curiosity she simulated, or really carried away by her newly-roused desires, nothing would do, but she must bring out and into the light the standing affair of her friend.

Those of my readers who have been placed in a similar position will readily understand the warmth of the grasp and the surprise of the look which greeted the first appearance in public of the new acquisition.

Bella beheld a man's member for the first time in her life, in the full plenitude of its power, and although it was not, I could plainly see, by any means a formidable one, yet its white shaft and redcapped head, from which the soft skin retreated as she pressed it, gained her quick inclination to learn more.

Charlie was equally moved; his eyes shone and his hand continued to rove all over the sweet young treasure of which he had taken possession.

Meanwhile the toyings of the little white hand upon the youthful member with which it was in contact had produced effects common under such circumstances to all of so healthy and vigourous a constitution as that of the owner of this particular affair.

Enraptured with the soft pressures, the geatle and delicious squeezings, and artless way in which the young lady pulled back the folds from the rampant nut, and disclosed the ruby crest, purple with desire, and the tip, ended by the tiny orifice, now awaiting its opportunity to send forth its slippery offering, the youth grew wild with lust, and Bella, participating in sensations new and strange, but which carried her away in a whirlwind of passionate excitement, panted for she knew not what of rapturous relief.

With her beautiful eyes half closed, her dewy lips parted, and her skin warm and glowing with the unwonted impulse stealing over her, she lay the delicious victim of whomsoever had the instant chance to reap her favours and pluck her delicate young rose.

Charlie, youth though he was, was not so blind as to lose so fair an opportunity; besides, his now rampant passions carried him forward despite the dictates of prudence which he otherwise might have heard.

He felt the throbbing and well-moistened centre quivering beneath his fingers, he beheld the beautiful girl lying invitingly to the amorous sport, he watched the tender breathings which caused the young breast to rise and fall, and the strong sensual emotions which animated the glowing form of his youthful companion.

The full, soft and swelling legs of the girl were now exposed to his sensuous gaze.

Gently raising the intervening drapery, Charlie still further disclosed the secret charms of his lovely companion until, with eyes of flame, he saw the plump limbs terminate in the full hips and white palpitating belly.

Then also his ardent gaze fell upon the centre spot of attraction—on the small pink slit which lay half hidden at the foot of the swelling mount of Venus, hardly yet shaded by the softest down.

The titillation which he had administered, and the caresses

which he had bestowed upon the coveted object had induced a flow of the native moisture which such excitement tends to provoke, and Bella lay with her peach-like slit well bedewed with nature's best and sweetest lubricant.

Charlie saw his chance. Gently disengaging her hand from its grasp upon his member, he threw himself frantically upon the recumbent figure of the girl.

His left arm wound itself round her slender waist, his hot breath was on her cheek, his lips pressed hers in one long, passionate and hurried kiss. His left hand, now free, sought to bring together those parts of both which are the active instruments of sensual pleasure, and with eager efforts he sought to complete conjunction.

Bella now felt for the first time in her life the magic touch of a man's machine between the tips of her rosy orifice.

No sooner had she perceived the warm contact which was occasioned by the stiffened head of Charlie's member, than she shuddered perceptibly, and already anticipating the delights of venery, gave down an abundance of proof of her susceptible nature.

Charlie was enraptured at his happiness, and eagerly strove to perfect his enjoyment.

But Nature, which had operated so powerfully in the development of Bella's sensual passions, left yet something to be accomplished, are the opening of so early a rosebud could be easily effected.

She was very young, immature, certainly so in the sense of those monthly visitations which are supposed to mark the commencement of puberty; and Bella's parts, replete as they were with perfection and freshness, were as yet hardly prepared for the accomodation of even so moderate a champion as that which, with round intruded head, now sought to enter in and effect a lodgment.

In vain Charlie pushed and exerted himself to press into the delicate parts of the lovely girl his excited member.

The pink folds and the tiny orifice withstood all his attempts to penetrate the mystic grotto. In vain the pretty Bella, now roused into a fury of excitement and half mad with the titillation she had already undergone, seconded by all the means in her power the audacious attempts of her young lover.

The membrane was strong and resisted bravely until, with a desperate purpose to win the goal or burst everything, the youth drew back for a moment, and then desperately plunging forward, succeeded in piercing the obstruction and thrusting the head and shoulders of his stiffened affair into the belly of the yelding girl.

Bella gave a little scream, as she felt the forcible inroad upon her secret charms, but the delicious contact gave her courage to bear the smart in hopes of the relief which appeared to be coming.

Meanwhile Charlie pushed again and again, and proud of the victory which he had already won, not only stood his ground, but at each thrust advanced some small way further upon his road.

It has been said, "ce n'est que le premier coup qui coute, "but it may be fairly argued that it is at the same time perfectly possible that "quelquefois il coute trop," as the reader may be inclined to infer with me in the present case.

Neither of our lovers, however, had strange to say, a thought on the subject, but fully occupied with the delicious sensations which had overpowered them, united

17

to give effect to those ardent movements which both could feel would end in ecstasy.

As for Bella, with her whole body quivering with delicious impatience, and her full red lips giving vent to the short excursive exclamations which announced the extreme gratification, she gave herself up body and soul to the dehghts of the coition. Her muscular compressions upon the weapon which had now effectually gained her, the firm embrace in which she held the writhing lad, the delicate tighs of the moistened, glove-like sheath, all tended to excite Charlie to madness. He felt himself in her body to the roots of his machine, until the two globes which tightened beneath the foaming champion of his manhood, pressed upon the firm cheeks of her white bottom. He could go no further and his sole employment was to enjoy—to reap to the full the delicious harvest of his exertions.

But Bella, insatiable in her passion, no sooner found the wished for junction completed, than relishing the keen pleasure which the stuff and warm member was giving her, became too excited to know or care further aught that was happenning, and her frenzied excitement, quickly overtaken again by the maddening spasms of completed lust, pressed downwards upon the object of her pleasure, threw up her arms in passionate rapture, and then sinking back in the arms of her lover, with low groans of ecstasic agony and little cries of surprise and delight, gave down a copious emission, which finding a reluctant escape below, inundated Charlie's balls.

No sooner did the youth witness the delivering enjoyment he was the means of bestowing upon the beautiful Bella, and became sensible of the flood which she had poured down in such profusion upon his person, then he was also seized with lustful fury. A raging forrent of desire seemed to rush through his veins; his instrument was now plunged to the hilt in her delicious belly, then, drawing back, he extracted the smoking member almost to the head. He pressed and bore all before him. He felt a tickling, maddening feeling creeping upon him; he tightened his grasp upon his young mistress, and at the same instant that another cry of rapturous enjoyment issued from her heaving breast, he found himself gasping upon her bosom, and pouring into her grateful womb a rich tickling jet of youthful vigour.

A low moan of salacious gratification escaped the parted lips of Bella, as she felt the jerking gushes of seminal fluid which came from the excited member within her; at the same moment the lustful frenzy of emission forced from Charlie a sharp and thrilling cry as he lay with upturned eyes in the last act of the sensuous drama.

That cry was the signal for an interruption which was as sudden as it was unexpected. From out the bordering shrubs there stole the sombre figure of a man and stood before the youthful lovers.

Horror froze the blood of both.

Slipping from his late warm and luscious retreat, and essaying as best he could to stand upright. Charlie recolled from the apparition as from some dreadful serpent.

As for the gentle Bella, no sooner did she catch sight of the intruder than, covering her face with her hands, she shrank back upon the seat which had been the silent witness of her pleasures, and too frightened to utter a sound, waited with what presence of mind she could assume to face the brewing storm.

Nor was she kept long in suspense.

Quickly advancing towards the guilty couple the newcomer seized the lad by the arm, while with a stern gesture of authority, he ordered him to repair the disorder of dress.

"Impudent boy," he hissed between his teeth, "what is is that you have done? To what lengths have your mad and savage passions hurried you? How will you face the rage of your justly offended father? How appease his angry resentment when in the exercise of my bounden duty. I apprise him of the mischief wrought by the hand of his only son."

As the speaker ceased, still holding Charlie by the wrist, he came forth into the moonlight and disclosed the figure of a man of some forty-five of age, short, stout, and somewhat corpulent. His face, decidedly handsome, was rendered still more attractive by a pair of brilliant eyes, which, black as jet, threw around fierce glances of passionate resentment. He was habited in a clerical dress, the sombre shades and quiet unobstructive neatness of which drew out only more prominently his remarkably muscular proportions and striking physiogomy.

Charlie appeared, as well, indeed, he might, covered with confusion, when to his infinite and selfish relief, the stern intruder turned to the young partner of his libidinous enjoyment.

"For you, miserable girl, I can only express my utmost horror and my most righteous indignation. Forgetful alike of the precepts of the holy mother church, careless of your honour, you have allowed this wicked and presumptuous boy to pluck the forbidden fruit? What now remains for you? Scorned by your friends, and driven from your uncle's house, you will herd with the beasts of the field, and Nebuchadnezar of old, shunned as centamination by your species, gladly gather a miserable sustenance in the highways. Oh, daughter of sin, child given up to lust and unto Satan. I say unto thee—''

The stranger had proceeded thus far in his abjuration of the unfortunate girl, when Bella, rising from her crouching attitude, threw herself at his feet, and joined her tears and prayers for forgiveness to those of her young lover.

"Say no more," at length continued the stern priest; "say no more. Confessions are of no avail, and humiliations do but add to your offence. My mind misgives me as to my duty in this sad affair, but if I obeyed the dictates of my present inclinations I should go straight to your natural guardians and acquaint them immediately with the infamous nature of my chance discovery."

"Oh, in pity, have mercy upon me," pleaded Bella, whose tears now coursed down her pretty cheeks, so lately aglow with wanton pleasure.

"Spare us, Father, spare us both. We will do anything in our power to make atonement. Six masses and several paters shall be performed on our account and our cost. The pilgrimage to the shrine of St. Engulphus, of which you spoke to me the other day, shall now surely be undertaken. I am willing to do anything, sacrifice anything, if you will spare this dear Bella."

The priest waived his hand for silence. Then he spoke, while accents of pity mingled with his naturally stern and resolute manner.

"Enough," said he, "I must have time. I must invoke assistance from the Blessed Virgin, who knew no sin, but who, without the carnal delights of mortal copulation, brought forth the babe of babes in the manger of Bethlehem. Come to me to-morrow in the sacristy, Bella. These in the precincts, I will unfold to you the Divine will concerning your transgression. At two o'clock I will expect you. As for you, rash youth, I shall reserve my judgment, and all action, until the following day, when at the same hour I shall likewise expect you.''

A thousand thanks were being poured out by the united throats of the penitents, when the Father warned them both to part.

The evening had long ago closed in, and the dews of night were stealing upwards.

''Meanwhile, good night and peace; your secret is safe with me, until we meet again,'' he spoke and disappeared,

CHAPTER II

Curiosity to learn the sequel of an adventure in which I already felt so much interest, as well as a tender solicitude for the gentle and amaible Bella, constrained me to keep in her vicinity, and I, therefore, took care not to annoy her with any very decided attentions on my part, or to raise resistance by an illtimed attack at a moment when it was necessary to the success of my design to remain within range of that young lady's operations.

I shall not attempt to tell of the miserable period passed by my young protegee in the interval which elapsed between the shocking discovery made by the holy Father Confessor, and the hour assigned by him for the interview in the sacristy, which was to decide the fate of the unfortunate Bella.

With trembling steps and downcast eyes the frightened girl presented herself at the porch and knocked.

The door was opened and the Father appeared upon the threshold.

At a sign Bella entered and stood before the stately presence of the holy man.

An embarrassing silence of some seconds followed. Father Ambrose was the first to break the spell.

"You have done right, my daughter, to come to me so punctually; the ready obedience of the penitent is the first sign of the spirit within which obtains the Divine forgiveness."

At these gracious words Bella took courage, and already a load seemed to fall from her heart.

Father Ambrose continued, seating himself at the same time upon the long-cushioned seat which covered a huge oak chest:

"I have thought much, and prayed much on your account, my daughter. For some time there appeared no way in which I could absolve my conscience otherwise than to go to your natural protector and lay before him the dreadful secret of which I have become the unhappy possessor."

Here he paused, and Bella, who knew well the severe character of her uncle, on whom she was entirely dependent, trembled at his words.

Taking her hand in his, and gently drawing the girl to the same seat, so that she found herself kneeling before him, while his right hand pressed her rounded shoulder, he went on:

"But I am wounded to think of the dreadful results which would follow such a disclosure, and I have asked for assistance from the Blessed Virgin in my trouble. She has pointed out a way which, while it also serves the ends of our holy church, likely prevents the consequences of your offence from being known to your uncle. The first necessity which this course imposes is, however, implicit obedience."

Bella, only too rejoiced to hear of a way out of her trouble, readily promised the most blind obedience to the command of her spiritual Father.

The young girl was kneeling at his feet. Father Ambrose bent his large head over her recumbent figure. A warm tint lit his cheeks, a strange fire danced in his fierce eyes: his hands trembled slightly, as they rested upon the shoulders of his penitent, but his composure was otherwise unruffled. Doubtless his spirit was troubled at the conflict going on within him between the duty he had to fulfil and the tortuous path by which he hoped to avoid the awful exposure.

The holy Father then began a long lecture upon the virtue of obedience, and the absolute submissions to the guidance of the minister of holy church.

Bella reiterated her assurances of entire patience and obedience in all things.

Meanwhile it was evident to me that the priest was a victim to some confined, but rebellious spirit which rose within him, and at times almost broke out into complete possession in the flashing eyes and hot passionate lips.

Father Ambrose gently drew the beautiful penitent nearer and nearer, until her fair arms rested upon his knees, and her face bent downwards in holy resignation, sunk almost unpon her hands.

"And now, my child," continued the holy man, "it is time that I should tell you the means vouschsafed to me by the Blessed Virgin by which alone I am absolved from exposing your offence. There are ministering spirits who have confided to them the relief of those passions and those exigencies which the servants of the church are forbidden openly to avow, but which, who can doubt, they have need to satisfy. These chosen few are mainly selected from among those who have already trodden the path of fleshly indulgence; to them is confined the solemn and holy duty of assuaging the earthly desires of our religious community in the strictest secrecy. To you," whispered the Father, his voice trembling with emotion, and his large hands passing by an easy transition from the shoulders of his penitent to her slender waist.

"To you, who have once already tasted the supreme pleasure of copulation, it is competent to assume this holy office. Not only will your sin be thus effaced and pardoned, but it will be permitted you to taste legitimately those ecstatic delights, those overpowering sensations of rapturous enjoyment, which in the arms of her faithful servants you are at all times sure to find. You will swim in a sea of sensual pleasure, without incurring the penalties of illicit love. Your absolution will follow each occasion of your yielding your sweet body to the gratification on the church, through her ministers, and you will be rewarded and sustained in the pious work by witnessing—nay, Bella, by sharing fully those intense and fervent emotions, the delicious enjoyment of your beautiful person must provoke."

Bella listened to this insidious proposal with mingled feelings of surprise and pleasure.

The wild and lewd impulses of her warm nature were at once awakened by the picture now presented to her fervid imagination—how could she hesitate?

The pious priest drew her yielding from towards him, and printed a long hot kiss upon her rosy lips.

"Holy Mother," murmured Bella, whose sexual instincts where each moment becoming more fully roused. "This is too much for me to bear—I long—I wonder—I know not what!"

"Sweet innocent, it will be for me to instruct you. In my person you will find your best and fittest preceptor in those exercices you will henceforth have to fulfil."

Father Ambrose slightly shifted his position. It was then that Bella noticed for the first time the heated look of sensuality which now almost frightened her.

It was now also that she became aware of the enormous protuberance of the front of the holy Father's silk cassock.

The excited priest hardly cared any longer to conceal either his condition or his designs.

Catching the beautiful child to his arms he kissed her long and passionately. He pressed her sweet body to his burly person, and rudely threw himself forward into closer contact with her graceful form.

At length the consuming lust with which he was burning carried him beyond all bounds, and partly releasing Bella from the constraint of his ardent embrace, he opened the front of his cassock, and exposed, without a blush, to the astonished eyes of his young penitent, a member the gigantic proportions of which, no less than its stiffness and rigidity completely confounded her.

It is impossible to describe the sensations produced upon

the gentle Bella by the sudden display of this formidable instrument.

Her eyes was instantly rivetted upon it, while the Father, noticing her astonishment, but detecting rightly that there was nothing mingled with it of alarm or apprehension, coolly placed it into her hands, It was then that Bella became wildly excited with the muscular contact of this tremendous thing.

Only having seen the very moderate proportions displayed by Charlie, she found her lewdest sensations quickly awakened by so remarkable a phenomenon, and glasping the huge object as well as she could in her soft little hands, she sank down beside it in an ectasy of sensual delight.

"Holy Mother, this is already heaven!" murmured Bella. "Oh! Father, who would have believed I could have been selected for such pleasure!"

This was too much for Father Ambrose. He was delighted at the lubricity of his fair penitent, and the success of his infamous trick (for he had planned the whole, and had been instrumental in bringing the two young lovers together and affording them an opportunity of indulging their warm temperaments, unknown to all save himself, as, hidden close by, with flaming eyes, he watched the amatory combat).

Hastily rising, he caught up the light figure of the young Bella, and placing her upon the cushioned seat on which he had lately been sitting, he threw up her plump legs and separating to the utmost her willing thighs, he beheld for an instant the delicious pinky slit which appeared at the bottom of her white belly. Then, without a word, he plunged his face towards it, and thrusting his lecherous tongue up the moist sheath as far as he could, he sucked it so deliciously that Bella, in a shuddering ecstasy of passion, her young body writhing in spasmodic contortions of pleasure, have down a plentiful emission, which the holy man swallowed like a custard.

For a few moments there was calm.

Bella lay on her back, her arms extended on either side, and her head thrown back in an attitude of delicious exhaustion, succeeding the wild emotions so lately occasioned by the lewd proceedings of the reverend Father.

Her bosom yet palpitated with the violence of her transports and her beautiful eyes remained half closed in languid repose.

Father Ambrose was one of the few who, under circumstances such as the present, was able to keep the instincts of passion under command. Long habits of patience in the attainment of his object, a general doggedness of manner and the conventional caution of his order, had not been lost upon his fiery nature, and although by nature unfitted for his holy calling, and a prey to desires as violent as they were irregular, he had taught himself to school his passions even to mortification.

It is time to lift the veil from the real character of this man. I do so with respect, but the truth must be told.

Father Ambrose was the living personification of lust. His mind was in reality devoted to its pursuit, and his grossly animal instincts, his ardent and vigorous constitution, no less than his hard unbending nature made him resemble in body, as in mind, the Satyr of old.

But Bella only knew him as the holy Father who had not only pardoned her offence, but who had opened to her the path by which she might, as she supposed, legitimately enjoy those pleasures which had already wrought so strongly on her young imagination.

The bold priest, singularly charmed, not only at the

success of his stratagem which had given into his hands so luscious a victim, but also at the extraordinary sensuality of her constitution, and the evident delight with which she lent herself to his desires, now set himself leisurely to reap the fruits of his trickery, and revel to the utmost in the enjoyment which the possession of all the delicate charms of Bella could procure to appease his frightful lust.

She was his at last, and as he rose from her quivering body, his lips yet reeking with the plentiful evidence of her participation in his pleasures, his member became yet more fearfully hard and swollen, and the dull red head shone with the bursting strain of blood and muscle beneath.

No sooner did the young Bella find herself released from the attack of her confessor upon the sensitive part of her person already described, and raised her head from the recumbent position into which it had fallen, than her eyes fell for the second time upon the big truncheon which the Father kept impudently exposed.

Bella noted the long and thick white shaft, and the curling mass of black hair out of which it rose, stiffly inclined upwards, and protruding from its end was the egg-shaped head, skinned and ruddy, and seeming to invite the contact of her hand.

Bella beheld this thickened muscular mass of stiffened flesh, and unable to resist the inclination, flew once more to seize it in her grasp.

She squeezed it,—she pressed it—she drew back the folding skin, and watched the broad nut, as it inclined towards her. She saw with wonder the small slit-like hole at its extremity and taking both her hands, she held it throbbing close to her face.

"Oh! Father, what a beautiful thing," exclaimed Bella, "what an immense one, too. Oh! Please, dear Father

Ambrose, do tell me what I must do to relieve you of those feelings which you say give our holy ministers of religion so much pain and uneasiness.

Father Ambrose was almost too excited to reply, but taking her hand in his, he showed the innocent girl how to move her white fingers up and down upon the shoulders of his huge aflair.

His pleasure was intense, and that of Bella was hardly less.

She continued to rub his limb with her soft palms and, looking up innocently to his face, asked softly—

"If that gave him pleasure, and was nice, and whether she might go on, as she was doing."

Meanwhile the reverend Father felt his big penis grow harder and even stiffer under the exciting titillations of the young girl.

"Stay a moment; if you continue to rub it so I shall spend," softly said he. "It will be better to defer it a little."

"Spend, my Father," asked Bella, eagerly, "what is that?"

"Oh, sweet girl, charming alike in your beauty and your innocence; how divinely you fulfil your divine mission," exclaimed Ambrose delighted to outrage and debase the evident inexperience of his young penitent.

"To spend is to complete the act whereby the full pleasure of venery is enjoyed, and then a rich quantity of thick white fluid escapes from the thing you now hold in your hand, and rushing forth, gives equal pleasure to him who ejects it and to the person who, in some manner or other, receives it."

Bella remembered Charlie and his ecstasy, and knew immediately what was meant.

"Would this outpouring give you relief, my Father?"

"Undoubtedly, my daughter; it is that fervent relief I have in view, offering you the opportunity of taking from me the blissful sacrifice of one of the humblest servants of the church."

"How delicious," murmured Bella; "by my means this rich stream is to flow, and all for me the holy man proposes this end of his pleasure—how happy I am to be able to give him so much pleasure."

As she half pondered, half uttered these thoughts she bent head down; a faint, but exquisitely sensual perfume rose from the object of her adoration. She pressed her moist lips upon its top, she covered the little slitlike hole with her lovely mouth, and imprinted upon the glowing member a fervent kiss.

"What is this fluid called?" asked Bella, once more raising her pretty face.

"It has various names," replied the holy man, "according to the status of the person employing them; but between you and me, my daughter, we shall call it spunk."

"Spunk!" repeated Bella, innocently, making the erotic word fall from her sweet lips with an unction which was natural under the circumstances.

"Yes, my, daughter, spunk is the word I wish you to understand it by, and you shall presently have a plentiful bedewal of the precious essence."

"How must I receive it?" enquired Bella, thinking of Charlie, and the tremendous difference relatively between his instrument and the gigantic and swollen penis in her presence now.

"There are, various ways, all of which you will have to learn, but at present we have only slight accomodation for the principal act of reverential venery, of that permitted copulation of which I have already spoken. We must, therefore, supply another and easier method, and instead of my discharging the essence called spunk into your body, where the extreme tightness of that little slit of yours would doubtless cause it to flow very abundantly, we will commence by the friction of your obedient fingers, until the time when I feel the approach of those spasms which accompany the emission. You shall then, at a signal from me, place as much as you can of the head of this affair between your lips, and there suffer me to disgorge the trickling spunk, until the last drop being expended I shall retire satisfied, at least for the time."

Bella, whose jealous instincts led her to enjoy the description which her confessor offered, and who was quite as eager as himself for the completion of this outrageous programme, readily expressed her willingness to comply.

Ambrose once more placed his large penis in Bella's fair hands.

Excited alike by the sight and touch of so remarkable an object, which both her hands now grasped with delight, the girl set herself to work to tickle, rub and press the huge and stiff affair in a way which gave the licentious priest the keenest enjoyment.

Not content with the friction or her delicate fingers, Bella, uttering words of devotion and satisfaction, now placed the foaming head upon her rosy lips and allowing it to slip in as far as it could, hoping by her touches, no less than by the gliding movements of her tongue, to provoke the delicious ejaculation of which she was in want.

This was almost beyond the auticipation of the holy priest, who had hardly supposed he should find so ready a disciple in the irregular attack he proposed; and his feelings being roused to the utmost by the delicious titillation he was now experiencing, prepared himself to flood the young girl's mouth and throat with the full stream of his powerful discharge.

Ambrose began to feel he could no last long without letting fly his roe, and thereby ending his pleasure.

He was one of those extraordinary men, the abundance of whose seminal ejaculation is far beyond that of ordinary beings. Not only had he the singular gift of repeatedly performing the veneral act with but very short respite, but the quantity with which he ended his pleasure was as tremendous as it was unusual. The superfluity seemed to come from him in proportion as his animal passions were aroused, and as his libidinous desires were intense and large, so also were the outpourings which relieved them.

It was under these circumstances that the gentle Bella undertook to release the pent-up torrents of this man's lust. It was her sweet mouth which was to be the recipient of those thick and slippery volumes of which she had had as yet not experience, and, all ignorant as she was of the effect of the relief she was so anxious to administer, the beautiful maid desired the consummation of her labour and the overflow of that spunk of which the good Father had told her.

Harder and hotter grew the rampant member as Bella's exciting lips pressed its large head and her tongue played around the little opening. Her two white hands bore back the soft skin from its shoulders and alternately tickled the lower extremity.

Twice Ambrose, unable to bear without spending the delicious contact, drew back the tip from her rosy lips.

At length Bella, impatient of delay, and apparently bent on perfecting her task, pressed forward with more energy than ever upon the stiff shaft.

Instantly there was a stiffening of the limbs of the good priest. His legs spread wide on either side of his penitent. His hand grasped convulsively at the cushions, his body was thrust forward and straightened out.

"Oh, holy Christ! I am going to spend!" he exclaimed, as with parted lips and glazing eyes he looked his last upon his innocent victim. Then he shivered perceptibly, and with low moans and short, hysteric cries, his penis, in obedience to the provocation of the young lady, began to jet forth its volumes of thick and glutinous fluid.

Bella, sensible of the gushes, which now came slopping jet, after jet, into her mouth, and ran in streams down her throat, hearing the cries of her companion, and perceiving with ready intuition that he was enjoying to the utmost the effect she had brought about, continued her rubbings and compression until gorged with the slimy discharge, and half choked by its abundance, she was compelled to let go of this human syringe, which continued to spout out its gushes in her face.

"Holy mother!" exclaimed Bella, whose lips and face were reeking with the Father's spunk. "Holy Mother? What pleasure I have had—and you, my Father, have I not given the precious relief you coveted?"

Father Ambrose, too agitated to reply, raised the gentle girl in his arms, and pressing her streaming mouth to his, sacked humid, kisses of gratitude and pleasure.

A quarter of an hour passed in tranquil repose uninterrupted by any signs of disturbance from without.

The door was fast, and the holy Father had well chosen his time.

Meanwhile Bella, whose desires had been fearfully excited by the scene we have attempted to describe, had conceived an extravagant longing to have the same operation performed upon her with the rigid member of Ambrose that she had suffered from the moderately proportioned weapon of Charlie.

Throwing her arms round the burly neck of her confessor, she whispered low words of invitation, watching, as she did so the effect in the already stiffening instrument between his legs.

"You told me that the tightness of this little slit," and here Bella placed his large hand upon it with a gentle pressure, "would make you discharge abundantly of the spunk you possess. What would I not give, my Father, to feel it poured into my body from the top of this red thing?"

It was evident how much the beauty of the young Bella, no less than the innocence and "naivete" of her character, inflamed the sensual nature of the priest. The knowledge of his triumph—of her utter helplessness in his hands—of her delicacy and refinement, all conspired to work to the extreme of lecherous desires of his fierce and wanton instincts. She was his. His to enjoy as he wished—his to break to every caprice of his horrid lust, and to bend to the indulgence of the most outrageous and unbridled sensuality.

"Ah, by heaven! it is too much," exclaimed Ambrose, whose lust, already rekindling, now rose violently into activity at this sollicitation. "Sweet girl, you don't know what you ask; the disproportion is terrible, and you would suffer much in the attempt."

"I would suffer all," replied Bella, "so that I could feel that fierce thing in my belly, and taste the gushes of its spunk up in me to the quick."

"Holy Mother of God! It is too much—you shall have it, Bella, you shall know the full measure of this stiffened machine, and, sweet girl, you shall wallow in an ocean of warm spunk.''

''Oh, my Father, what heavenly bliss!''

''Strip, Bella, remove everything that can interfere with our movements, which I promise you will be violent enough.''

Thus ordered, Bella was soon divested of her clothing, and finding her Confessor appeared charmed at the display of her beauty, and that his member swelled and lengthened in proportion as she exhibited her nudity, she parted with the last vestige of drapery, and stood as naked as she was born.

Father Ambrose was astonished at the charms which now faced him. The full hips, the budding breasts, the skin as white as snow and soft as satin, the rounded buttocks and swelling thighs, the flat white belly and lovely mont covered only with the thinnest down; and above all the charming pinky slit which now showed itself at the bottom of the mount, now hid timorously away between the plump thighs and with a snort of rampant lust he fell upon his victim.

Ambrose glasped her in his arms. He pressed her soft and glowing form to his burly front. He covered her with his salacious kisses, and giving his lewd tongue full licence, promised the young girl all the joys of Paradise by the introduction of his big machine within her slit and belly.

Bella met him with a little cry of ecstasy, and as the excited ravisher bore her backwards to the couch, already felt the broad and glowing head of gigantic penis pressing against the warm moist lips of her almost virgin orifice.

And now, the holy man finding delight in the contact of his penis with the warm lips of Bella's slit, began pushing it in between with all his energy until the big nut was covered with the moisture which the sensitive little sheath exuded.

Bella's passions were at fever height. The efforts of Father Ambrose to lodge the head of his member within the moist lips of her little slit, so far from deterring her, spurred her to madness until, with another faint cry, she fell prone and gushed down the slippery tribute of her lascivious temperament.

This was exactly what the bold priest wanted, and as the sweet warm emission bedewed his fiercely distended penis, he drove resolutely in, and at one bound sheathed half its ponderous length in the beautiful child.

No sooner did Bella feel the stiff entry of the terrible member within her tender body, than she lost all the little control of herself she had, and setting aside all thought of the pain she was enduring, she wound her legs about his loins, and entreated her huge assaillant not to spare her.

"My sweet and delicious child," whispered the salacious priest, "my arms are round you, my weapon is already half way up your tight little belly. The joys of Paradise will be yours presently."

"Oh, I know it; I feel it, do not draw back, give me the delicious thing as far as you can."

"There, then, I push, I press, but I am far too largely made to enter you easily. I shall burst you, possibly; but it is now too late. I must have you—or die."

Bella's parts relaxed a little, and Ambrose pushed in another inch. His throbbing member lay skinned and soaking, pushed half way into the little girl's belly. His pleasure was most intense, and the head of his instrument was compressed deliciously by Bella's slit.

"Go on, dear Father, I am waiting for the spunk you promised me."

It little needed this stimulant to induce the confessor to an exercice of his tremendous powers of copulation. He pushed frantically forward; he plunged his hot penis still further and further at each effort, and then with one huge stroke buried himself to the balls in Bella's light little person.

It was then that the furious plunge of the brutal priest became more than his sweet victim, sustained as she had been by her own advanced desires, could endure.

With a faint shrick of physical anguish, Bella felt that her ravisher had burst through all the resistance which her youth had opposed to the entry of his member, and the torture of the forcible insertion of such a mass bore down the prurient sensations with which she had commenced to suport the attack.

Ambrose cried aloud in rapture, he looked down upon the fair thing his serpent had stung. He gloated over the victim now impaled with the full rigour of his huge rammer. He felt the maddening contact with inexpressible delight. He saw her quivering with the anguish of his forcible entry. His brutal nature was fully aroused. Come what might he would enjoy to his utmost, so he wound his arms about the beautiful girl and treated her to the full measure of his burly member.

"My beauty! you are indeed exciting, you must also enjoy. I will give you the spunk I spoke of, but I must first work up my nature by this luscious titillation. Kiss me, Bella, then you shall have it, and while the hot spunk leaves me and enters your young parts, you shall be sensible of the throbbing joys I also am experiencing. Press, Bella, let me push, so, my child, now it enters again. Oh! oh!"

Ambrose raised himself a moment, and noted the immense shaft round which the pretty slit of Bella was now intensely stretched.

Firmly embedded in his luscious sheath, and keenly relishing the exceeding tightness of the warm folds of youthful flesh which now encased him, he pushed on, unmindful of the pain his tormenting member was producing, and only anxious to secure as much enjoyment to himself as he could. He was not a man to be deterred by any false notions of pity in such a case, and now pressed himself inwards to his utmost, while his hot lips sucked delicious kisses from the open and quivering lips of the poor Bella.

For some minutes nothing now was heard but the jerking blows with which the lascivious priest continued his enjoyment, and the cluck, cluck of his huge penis, as it alternately entered and retreated in the belly of the beautiful penitent.

It was not to be supposed that such a man as Ambrose was ignorant of the tremendous powers of enjoyment his member could rouse within one of the opposite sex, and that with its size and disgorging capabilities of such a nature as to enlist the most powerful emotions in the young girl in whom he was operating.

But Nature was asserting herself in the person of the young Bella. The agony of the stretching was fast being swallowed up in the intense sensations of pleasure produced by the vigorous weapon of the holy man, and it was not long before the low moans and sobs of the pretty child became mingled with expressions, half choked in the depth of her feelings, expressive of delight.

"Oh, my Father! Oh, my dear, generous Father! Now, now push. Oh! push. I can bear—I wish for it. I am in heaven! The blessed instrument is so hot in its head. Oh! my heart. Oh! my—oh! Holy Mother, what is this I feel?"

Ambrose saw the effect he was producing. His own pleasure advanced apace. He drove steadily in and out, treating Bella to the long hard shaft of his member up to the crisp hair which covered his big balls, at each forward thrust.

At length Bella broke down, and treated the electrified and ravished man with a warm emission which ran all over his stiff affair.

It is impossible to describe the lustful frenzy which now took possession of the young and charming Bella. She clung with desperate tenacity to the burly figure of the priest, who bestowed upon the heaving and voluptuous body the full force and vigour of his manly thrust. She held him in her tight and slippery sheath to his balls.

But in her ecstasy Bella never lost sight of the promised perfection of the enjoyment. The holy man was to spend his spunk in her as Charlie had done, and the thought added fuel to her lustful fire.

When, therefore, Father Ambrose, throwing his arms close round her taper waist, drove up his stallion penis to the very hairs in Bella's slit, and sobbing, whispered that the ''spunk'' was coming at last, the excited girl straightway opening her legs to the utmost, with positive shrieks of pleasure let him send his pent-up fluid in showers into her very vitals.

Thus he lay for full two minutes, while at each hot and forcible injection of the slippery semen, Bella gave plentiful evidence by her writhings and cries of ecstasy the powerful discharge was producing.

CHAPTER III

I do not think I ever felt my unfortunate infirmity in the matter of a natural inability to blush more acutely than on the present occasion. But even a flea might have blushed at the wanton sight which thrust itself upon his vision on the occasion I have herein recorded. So young, so apparently innocent a girl, and yet so lewd, so lascivious in her inclinations and desires. A person of infinite freshness and beauty—a mind of flaming sensuality fanned by the accidental course of events into an active volcano of lust.

Well might I have exclaimed with the poet of old:

"O Moses!" or with the more practical descendant of the Patriarch: "Holy Moses!"

It is needless to speak of the change which Bella's whole being underwent after such experiences as these I have related. They were manifest and apparent in her carriage and demeanour.

What became of her youthful lover I never knew nor cared to inquire, but I am led to believe that holy Father Ambrose was not insensible to those irregular tastes which are so largely ascribed to his order, and that the youth was led by easy stages to lend "himself," no less than his young mistress to the gratification of the insensate desires of the priest.

But to return to my own observations so far as they extended to the fair Bella.

Although a Flea cannot blush, we can "observe" and I have taken upon me to commit to pen and ink all those amatory passages in my experiences which I think may interest the seeker after truth. We can write, at least this Flea can, or else these pages would not now be before the reader, and that is enough.

It was several days before Bella found an opportunity of again visiting her clerical admirer, but at length the chance come, and, as might be expected, she quickly availed herself of it.

She had found means to apprise Ambrose of her intention of visiting him, and that astute individual was accordingly ready to receive his pretty guest as before.

Bella no sooner found herself alone with her seducer than she threw herself into his arms, and pressing his huge carcass to her little form, lavished upon him the most tender caresses.

Ambrose was not slow in returning to the full the warmth of her embrace, and thus it happened that the pair found themselves hotly engaged in the exchange of burning kisses, and reclining face to face upon the well-cushioned seat before alluded to.

But Bella was not likely now to be contented with kisses only, she desired more solid fare, which she knew from experience the Father could give her.

Ambrose, on his part, was no less excited. His blood flowed quickly, his dark eye flamed with unconcealed lust, and his protuberant dress displayed only too plainly the disorder of his senses.

Bella perceived his condition; neither his inflamed looks, nor the evident erection, which he took no trouble to conceal, escaped her—she sought to add to his desires, if possible, not to diminish them.

Soon, however, Ambrose showed her that he required no further incentive, for he deliberately produced his fiercely distended weapon in a state the bare sight of which drove Bella frantic with desire. At any other time Ambrose would have been more prudent of his pleasures than thus early to have proceeded to work with his celicious little conquest. On this occasion, however, his senses ran riot with him, and he was unable to check the overwhelming desire to revel at once and as soon as possible in the juvenile charms thus offered him.

He was already upon her body. His great bulk covered her figure most powerfully and completely. His distended member bore hardly against Bella's stomach, and her clothes were already raised to her waist.

With a trembling hand Ambrose seized the centre chink

of his wishes—eagerly he brought the hot and crimson tip towards its moist and opening lips. He pushed, he strove to penetrate—he succeeds; the immense machine slowly but surely enters—already the head and shoulders have disappeared.

A few steady, deliberate thrusts complete the conjunction, and Bella has received the whole length of Ambrose's huge excited member in her body.

The ravisher lay panting upon her bosom in complete possession of her inmost charms.

Bella, into whose little belly the vigorous mass was thus crammed, felt most powerfully the effects of the throbbing and hot intruder.

Meanwhile Ambrose began to thrust up and down. Bella threw her white arms around his neck, and twined her pretty silk clad legs all wantonly above his loins.

"How delicious," murmured Bella, kissing rapturously his thick lips, "Push me—push up me harder. Oh, how it forces me open—how large it is! How hot—how—oh my—oh!"

And down came a shower from Bella's storehouse, in response to the strong thrusts received, while her head fell back and her mouth opened in the spasms of coition.

The priest restrained himself, he paused an instant, the throbbing of his long member sufficiently announced his condition; he wished to prolong his pleasure to the utmost.

Bella squeezed the terrible shaft in her inermost person, and felt it grow harder and even stiffer while its purple head pressed up to her young womb.

Almost immediately afterwards her unwieldy lover, unable to prolong his pleasure, succumbed to the intensest of keen and all pervading sensation of glutinous fluid.

"Oh, it is coming from you," cried the excited girl. "I

feel it in gushes. Oh! give it me—more—more—pour it into me—push harder; do not spare me! Oh, another gush! Push—tear me if you like—but let me have all your spunk."

I have before spoken of the quantity Father Ambrose possessed the power of discharging, and he now surpassed himself. He had been bottled up for nearly a week, and Bella now received such a tremendous stream of his nature that his discharge more resembled the action of a syringe than the outpouring from the genitals of man.

At last Ambrose dismounted, and Bella on standing once more upon her feet, felt a clinging slippery stream trickling slowly down her plump thighs.

Hardly had the Father withdrawn than the door leading into the church opened, and, behold, two other priests presented themselves within its portal. Concealment was of course impossible.

"Ambrose," exclaimed the elder of the two, a man apparently between thirty and forty years old, "this is against our rules and privileges, which enact that all such game shall be in common."

"Take it then," growled the person addressed. "It is not too late—I was going to tell you of what I had got, only—"

"Only the delicious temptation of this young mossrose was too much for you, my friend!" exclaimed the other, seizing, as he spoke, upon the astonished Bella, and forcing his large hand up her clothes to her soft thighs.

"I saw it all through the keyhole," whispered the brute in her ear. "You need not be frightened, we shall only treat you the same, my dear."

Bella remembered the conditions of her admittance to the solace of the church, and supposed this was only a part of her new duties. She therefore rested unresistingly in the arms of the two new comers.

Meanwhile his companion had passed his strong arm around Bella's waist, and covered her delicate cheek with kisses.

Ambrose looked stupid and confounded.

The young lady thus found herself between two fires, to say nothing of the smouldering passion of her original possessor. In vain she looked from one to the other for some respite, some means of extrication from her predicament.

For, be it known, that although she fully resigned herself to the position into which the cunning of Father Ambrose had consigned her, a bodily feeling of weakness and fear of the new assailants nearly overcame her.

Bella read nothing but lust and raging desire in the looks of the new-comers, while the non-resistance of Ambrose disarmed all thought of defence on her own part.

The two men had now got her between them, and while the first speaker had pushed his hand as far as her rosy slit, the other lost no time in possessing himself of the well-rounded cheeks of her plump buttocks.

Between them Bella was powerless to resist.

"Stay a moment," at length suggested Ambrose, "if you are in earnest to enjoy her, at least undress without tearing her clothes to pieces, as you both seemed inclined to do."

"Strip, Bella," continued he, "we must all share you, it seems; so prepare to become the willing instrument of our united pleasures."

"Our convent contains others no less exigent than myself, and your office will be no sinecure, so you had better remember always the privileges you are called upon to fulfil, and be ready to relieve these holy men of the fiery desires which you yet know how to assuage.''

Thus directed there was no alternative.

Bella stood naked before the three vigorous priests.

Murmurs of delight burst from all when Bella stood timidly forth in her beauty.

No sooner did the spokesman of the newcomers, who was evidently the superior of thet three, perceive the beautiful nudity now presented to his passionate glances, without any hesitation, he opened his dress, and giving liberty to a large and long member, caugnt the beautiful girl in his arms, bore her back to the couch, and then, spreading open her pretty thighs, he planted himself between, and hastily bringing the head of his raging champion to the soft orifice, thrust forward, and at one bound buried himself to his balls.

Bella gave a little cry of ecstasy, as she felt the stiff insertion of this new and powerful weapon.

To the man in full possession of the beautiful child the contact was ecstasy, and the feeling with which he found himself completely buried in her body to the hilt of his rampant penis was one of undefiniable emotion. He had no idea he should so readily penetrate her young parts, but he had omitted to take into account the flood of semen which she had already received.

The Superior, however, gave her no time for reflection, but commenced to run his course so energetically that his long and powerful strokes produced their fullest effects upon her warm temperament, and almost immediatly coused her to give down her sweet emission,

This was too much for the wanton ecclesiastic. Already firmly imbedded in the tight and glove-like sheath, he no sooner felt the hot effusion than he uttered a long growl, and discharged furiously.

Bella relished the spouting torrent of the strong man's lust, and throwing out her legs, received him to his utmost length in her belly, allowing him there to satiate lust in the jetting streams of his fiery nature.

Bella's lewdest feelings were roused by this second and determined attack upon her person, and her excitable nature received with exquisite delight the rich libations the two stalwart champions had pourced out. But prurient as she was, the young lady found herself much exhausted by this continued strain upon her bodily powers, and it was therefore with dismay that she perceived the second of the intruders preparing to take advantages of the retirement of the Superior.

But what was Bella's astonishment to discover the gigantic proportions of the Priest who now presented himself. Already his dress was in disorder and before him stood stiffly erected a member before which even the vigorous Ambrose was forced to cede.

Out of a curling fringe of red hair sprang the white column of flesh, capped by the shining dull red head, the tight and closely, shut orifice of which looked, as if it was obliged to be careful and to prevent a premature over flow of its juices.

Two huge and hairy balls hung closely below, and completed the picture, at sight of which Bella's blood began once more to boil, and her youthful spirits to expand with longing for the disproportionate combat.

''Oh! my Father, how shall I ever get that great thing into my poor little person?'' asked Bella, in dismay, ''How shall I be able to endure it, when it does go in! I fear it will hurt me dreadfully!''

"I will be very careful, my daughter. I will go slowly. You are well prepared now by the juices of the holy men who have had the good fortune to precede me."

Bella fingered the gigantic penis.

The Priest was ugly in the extreme. He was short and stout, but built with shoulders broad enough for a Hercules.

The child had caught a sort of lewd madness; his ugliness only served further to rouse her sensual desires; her hands could not meet round his member. She continued, however, to hold it, to press it and unconsciously to bestow upon it caresses which increased its rigidity and advanced the pleasure. It stood like a bar of iron in her soft hands.

Another moment and the third assailant was upon her, and Bella, almost equally excited, strove to impale herself upon the terrible weapon.

For some minutes the feat seemed impossible, well lubricated as she was by the previous overflowings she had received.

At length a furious lunge drove in the enormous head.

Bella uttered a cry of real anguish; another, and another lunge, the brutal wretch, blind to all but his own gratification, continued to penetrate.

Bella cried out in her agony, and wildly strove to detach herself from her fierce assailant.

Another thrust, another cry from his victim, and the priest had penetrated her to the quick.

Bella had fainted.

The two observers of this monstrous act of debauchery seemed at first inclined to interfere, but it seemed as if they experienced a cruel pleasure in witnessing the conflict, and certainly their lewd movements, and the interest they evidently took in observing the minutest details argued their satisfaction.

I draw a veil over the scene of lust which followed, over the writhings of the savage, as he—securely in possession of the person of the young and beautiful child—slowly spun out his enjoyment, until his gross and fervid discharge put an end to his ecstasies, and allowed an interval in which to restore the poor girl to life.

The stalwart Father had discharged twice before he drew out his long and reeking member, and the volume of spunk which followed was such as to fall pattering in a pool upon the wooden floor.

At length sufficiently recovered to move, the young Bella was permitted to perform those ablutions which the streaming condition of her delicate parts rendered necessary.

CHAPTER IV

Several bottles of wine, of old and rare vintage, were now produced, and under their potent influence, Bella slowly recovered her strength.

Within an hour the three priests, finding that she was now sufficiently restored to entertain their lascivious advances, once more began to show signs of a desire for a further enjoyment of her person.

Excited no less by the generous wine than by the sight and touch of her lewd companions, the girl now commenced to pull from their cassocks, and to uncover the members of the three priests, whose enjoyment of the scene was evidently manifested by their absence of restraint.

In less than a minute Bella had all three of their long and stiff affairs in full view. She kissed and toyed with them, sniffing the faint fragrance which arose from them, and fingering the blushing shafts with all the eagerness of an accomplished Cyprian.

"Let us fuck," piously ejaculated the Superior, whose prick was at that moment at Bella's lips.

"Amen," chanted Ambrose.

The third ecclesiastic was silent, but his huge penis menaced the skies.

Bella was directed to choose her first assailant in this new round. She selected Ambrose, but the Superior supervened.

Meanwhile, the doors being secured, the three priests deliberately stripped themselves, and thus presented to the brilliant gaze of the youthful Bella three vigorous champions in the prime of life, each armed with a stalwart weapon, which stood once more firmly in their fronts and wagged about threateningly as they moved.

"Oh, fie! What monsters!" exclaimed the young lady, whose shame, however, did not prevent her handling alternately these redoubtable engines.

They have sat her upon the edge of the table, and one by one they sucked her young parts, rolling their hot tongues round and round in the moist red slit in which all had so recently appeased their lust. Bella lent herself to this with joy, and opened to the utmost her plump legs to gratify them.

"I propose she shall suck us one after the other," exclaimed the Superior.

"Certainly," assented Father Clement, the man of the red hair and huge erection. "But not to finish so. I want her once more in the belly."

"No; certainly not, Clement," said the Superior. "You have well nigh split her in two as it is; you must finish down her throat or not all."

Bella had no intention of again submitting to an attack from Clement, so she cut short the discussion by seizing on the fat member and putting as much of it as she could into her pretty mouth.

Up and down the blue nut the girl worked her soft moist lips, every now and then pausing to receive as much of it as possible within her mouth. Her fair hands passed around the long, large shaft, and clutched it in a tremulous embrace, as she watched the monstrous penis swell harder with the intensity of the sensations imparted by her delicious touches.

In less than five minutes Clement began to utter howlings more like those of a wild beast than the exclamations of the human lungs, and spent in volumes down her gullet.

Bella drew down the skin along the long shaft, and encouraged the flood to end.

Clement's spendings were as thick and hot as they were plentiful, and squirt after squirt of spunk flew into the girl's mouth.

Bella swallowed it all.

"There is a new experience I must now instruct you, in my daughter," said the Superior, as Bella next applied her soft lips to his burning member.

"You will find it productive of more pain than pleasure at first, but the ways of Venus are difficult, and only to be learnt and enjoyed by degrees."

"I shall submit myself to all, my Father," replied the girl; I know my duty now better, and that I am one of those favoured ones selected to relieve the desires of the good Fathers."

"Certainly, my daughter, and you feel the bliss of heaven in advance while obeying our slightest wishes, and indulging all our inclinations, however strange and irregular they may be."

With that he took the girl in his strong arms, and bore her once more to the couch, where he placed her on her face, thus exposing her naked and beautiful posteriors to the whole three.

Next, placing himself between the thighs of his victim, he pointed the tip of his stiff member at the small orifice between Bella's plump buttocks, and pushing forward his well-lubricated weapon by slow degrees, at the same time began to penetrate her in this novel and unnatural manner.

"Oh,—my!—" cried Bella, "you are in the wrong place—it hurts.—Pray—oh! Pray—ah! Have mercy. Oh! pray spare me! Holy Mother! I die!"

This last exclamation was caused by a final and vigorous thrust on the part of the Superior, which sent his stallion member up to the hairs that covered the lower portion of his belly—Then Bella felt that he was up her body to his balls.

Passing his strong arm around her hips, he pressed close to her back; his stout belly rubbed against her buttocks, and his stiff member was kept thrust into her rectum as far as it would go. The pulsations of pleasure were evident throughout its swollen length, and Bella, biting her lips, awaited the movements of the man which she well knew he was about to commence in order to finish his enjoyment.

The other two priests looked on with envious lust, slowly frigging their big members the while.

As for the Superior, maddened by the tightness of this new and delicious sheath, he laboured at her round buttocks until, with a final lunge, he filled her bowels with his hot discharge. Then drawing his instrument, still erect and smoking, from her body, he declared that he had opened up a new route to pleasure, and recommended Ambrose to avail himself of it.

Ambrose, whose feelings during this time may be better imagined than described, was now rampant with desire.

The sight of his confreres enjoying themselves gradually produced a state of erotic excitement within him that it became necessary to quench as soon as possible.

"Agreed," he cried, "I will enter by the Temple of Sodom, and you, meanwhile, shall fill with your sturdy sentinel the Halls of Venus."

"Say rather of legitimate enjoyment," rejoined the Superior with a grin. "Be it as you say; I should well like another taste of so tight a belly."

Bella still lay upon her belly upon the couch: Her rounded posterior fully exposed, more dead than alive from the brutal attack which she had just suffered. Not a drop of the semen which had been injected into her so plentifully escaped from the dark recess, but below her slit still ran with the combined emission of the priests. Ambrose seized her.

Placed accross the thighs of the Superor, Bella now found his still vigorous member knocking against the lips of her pink slit; slowly she guided it in, as she lowered herself upon it. Presently it all entered—she had it to the roots.

But now the vigorous Superior, passing his arms around

her waist, drew her down upon him, and sinking backwards, brought her large and exquisite buttocks before the angry weapon of Ambrose, who straightway bore directly at the already well moistened aperture between their hillocks.

A thousand difficulties presented themselves to be overcome, but at length the lecherous Ambrose felt himself buried in the entrails of his tender victim.

Slowly he drew his member up and down the slippery channel. He spun out his pleasure and enjoyed the vigorous bounds with which his Superior was treating the fair Bella in front.

Presently, with a deep sigh, the Superior reached his climax, and Bella felt him rapidly filling her slit with spunk.

She could not resist the impetus, and her own overflowing mingled with those of her assailant.

Ambrose, however, had husbanded his resources, and now held the pretty girl in front of him, firmly impaled upon his huge affair.

In this position Clement could not resist the opportunity, but watching his chance while the Superior was wiping his person, he drove himself in front of Bella, and almost immediately succeeded in penetrating her belly, now liberally bedewed with their slippery leavings.

Enormous though it was, Bella found means to receive the red-haired monster which now stretched her delicate body with its entire length, and for the next few minutes nothing was heard but the sighs and lustful moans of the combattants.

Presently their motions grew harder; Bella expected every moment would be her last. The huge member of Ambrose was up her posterior passage to his balls, while the gigantic truncheon of Clement made all froth again within her belly.

The child was supported between the two, her feet fairly off the ground, and, subject, to the blows, first in front and then behind, with which the priests worked their excited engines in their respective channels.

Just as Bella commenced to lose her consciousness, she became aware by the heavy breathing and the tremendous stiffness of the brute in front that his discharge was coming and the next moment she felt the hot injection flow from the gigantic prick in strong and viscid jets.

"Ah! I spend" cried Clement, and with that he squirted a copious flood up little Bella, to her infinite delight.

"Mine's coming too," shrieked Ambrose, driving home his vigorous member, and pouring a hot jet of his spunk into Bella's bowels at the same time.

Thus the two continued disgorging the prolific contents of their bodies into that of the gentle girl, while she experienced the double flood, and swam in a deluge of delights.

Anyone would have supposed that a flea of average intelligence only would have had enough of such disgusting exhibitions as I have thought it my duty to disclose; but a certain feeling of friendship as well as sympathy for the young Bella impelled me still to remain in her company.

The event justified my anticipations, and as will hereafter appear, determined my future movements.

Three days only elapsed ere the young lady met the three priests by appointment in the same place.

On this occasion, Bella had taken extra care in regard to her toilet, and the result was that she now appeared more enchanting than ever, in the prettiest of silk dresses, the tightest of kid-boots, and the tiniest of lovely and well-fitting gloves.

The three men were in raptures, and Bella was received in so warm a manner that already her young blood mounted hot to her face with desire.

The door was promptly secured, and then down went the nether garments of the reverend fathers, and Bella, amid the mingled caresses and lascivious touches of the trio, beheld their members baldy exposed and already menacing her.

The Superior was the first who advanced with the intention of enjoying her.

Boldly placing himself in front of her little form, he bore roughly against her, and taking her in his arms, covered her mouth and face with hot kisses.

Bella's excitement equalled his.

By their desire, Bella denuded herself of her drawers and petticoats, and retaining only her exquisite dress, silk stockings, and pretty kid-boots, offered herself to their admiration and lascivious touches.

A moment later and the Father, sinking deliciously upon her reclining figure, had pushed himself to the hairs in her young charms, and remained soaking in the tight conjunction with evident gratification.

Pushing, squeezing, and rubbing against her, the Superior commenced delicious movements, which had the effect of raising both his partner's susceptibilities and his own. His prick, in its increased size and hardness, bore evidence of this.

"Push, oh! Push me harder," murmured Bella.

Meanwhile Ambrose and Clement whose desires could ill brook the delay, sought to engage some portion of the girl's attention.

Clement put his huge member into her soft white hand and Ambrose, nothing daunted, mounting on the couch, brought the tip of his bulky affair to her delicate lips.

After a few moments, the Superior withdrew from his luscious position.

Bella rose upon the edge of the couch. Before her were the three men, each had his member exposed and erect before him, and the enormous head of Clement's engine turned back almost against his fat belly.

Bella's dress was raised to her waist, her legs and thighs were in full view, and between them the luscious, pinky slit, now reddened and excited by the too abrupt insertion and withdrawal of the Superior's prick.

"Stay a moment," he observed; "let us proceed with order in our pleasures. This beautiful child is to satisfy all three, therefore it will be necessary to regulate both our enjoyments, and also to enable her to support the attacks to which she will be liable. For myself I do not care whether I come first or second; but as Ambrose spends like an ass, will probably make all smoke again in the regions he penetrates, I propose to pass first. Certainly Clement must be content with the second or third place, or his enormous member would not only split the girl, but what is of far more consequence, spoil our pleasure."

"I was third last time." exclaimed Clement. "I see no reason why I should always be last. I claim the second place."

"Good, so let it be then," cried the Superior. "You, Ambrose, will have a slippery nest for your share."

"Not I," rejoined that determined ecclesiastic; "if you go first, and that monster Clement has her second, and before me, I shall attack "by the breech" and pour offering in another direction."

"Do with me as you will," cried Bella, "I will try and bear all. But, oh, my Fathers, make haste and began."

Once more the Superior drove in his stalwart weapon. Bella met the siff insertion with delight. She hugged him, she bore down against him, and received his jets of emission with ecstatic outbursts of her own.

Clement now presented himself. His monstrous affair was already between the plump legs of the young Bella. The disproportion was terrible, but the priest was as strong and lewd as largely made, and after sundry violent and ineffectual efforts, he got in and commenced to ram the whole of his asinine member into her belly.

It is impossible to relate how the terrible proportions of this man roused the lescivious imaginations of Bella, or with what a frenzy of passion she found herself deliciously crammed and stretched by the huge genitals of Father Clement.

After a struggle of full ten minutes, Bella received the throbbing mass up to the big balls, which pressed her bottom below.

Bella threw out both her pretty legs, and allowed the brute to revel at his leisure in her charms.

Clement showed no anxiety to cut short his luscious enjoyment, and it was a quarter of an hour before two violent discharges put an end to his pleasure.

Bella received them with deep sighs of delight, and gave down a copious emission of her own upon the thick inpourings of the lustful Father.

Clement had hardly withdrew his monstrous affair from the belly of the young Bella, then, reeking from the arms of her huge lover, she fell into those of Ambrose.

True to his expressed intention, it is now her beautiful buttocks he attacks, and seeks with fierce energy to insert the throbbing head of his instrument within the tender folds of her posterior's aperture.

In vain he seeks to gain a lodgment. The broad head of his weapon is repulsed at each assault, as with brutal lust he tries hard to force himself inwards.

But Ambrose is not to be so easily defeated, he essays again, and at length a determined effort lodges the head within the delicate opening.

Now is his time—a vigorous lunge drives in a couple of inches more and with a single bound the lascivious priest then buries himself to the balls.

Bella's beautiful buttocks had a decided attraction for the lustful priet. He was agitated to an extraordinary degree, as he bore forward in his fierce efforts. He pressed his long and thick member inwards with ecstasy, regardless of the pain the stretching was causing her, as long as he could feel the delicious constrictions of her delicate young parts.

Bella utters a dreadful cry. She is impaled upon the stiff member of the brutal ravisher. She feels his throbbing flesh in her vitals, and endeavours, with frantic efforts, to escape.

But Ambrose, passing his strong arms round her slender waist, restrains her, while he follows each movement made by her, and retains himself in her quivering body by a continued inward strain.

Thus struggling, step by step, the girl crossed the appartment, having the fierce Ambrose firmly imbedded in her posterior passage.

Meanwhile this lewd spectacle was not without its effect upon the beholders.

A shout of laughter issued from their throats, and both applauded the vigour of their companion, whose visage, inflamed and working, bore ample testimony to his pleasurable emotions.

But the sight also quickly roused their desires, and both showed by the state of their members that they were as yet by no means satisfied.

Bella having by this time arrived close to the Superior, the latter caught her in his arms, and Ambrose, taking advantage of this timely check, commenced to push his member about in her bowels, while the intense heat of her body afforded him the liveliest pleasure.

By the position in which the three were now placed, the Superior found his mouth on a level with Bella's natural charms, and instantly glueing his lips thereto, he sucked her moistened slit.

But the excitement thus occasioned required more solid enjoyment, and drawing the pretty girl across his knees as he sat upon his seat, he let loose his bursting member and quickly drove it into her soft belly.

Thus Bella was between two fires, and the fierce thrusts of Father Ambrose upon her plump buttocks were now supplemented by the fervid efforts of the Superior in the other direction.

Both revelled in a sea of sensual delights, both bathed themselves to the full in the delicious sensations they experienced, while their victim, perforated before and behind by their swelling members, had to sustain as she could their excited movements.

But a further trial awaited the young Bella, for no sooner did the vigorous Clement witness the close conjunction of his companions, than, inflamed with envy, and stung by the violence of his passions, he mounted the seat behind the superior, and taking possesssion of poor Bella's head, presented his flaming weapon against her rosy lips, then forcing the tip, with the narrow aperture already exuding anticipatory drops, into her pretty mouth, he made her rub the long, hard shaft in her hand.

Meanwhile Ambrose found the insertion of the Superior's member in front quickly bring on his proceedings, while the latter, equally excited by the back action of his comrade, speedily began to feel the approaches of the spasms preceding and accompanying the final act of emission.

Clement was the first to let fly, and he sent his glutinous discharge in showers down the throat of the little Bella.

Ambrose followed, and falling on her back shot a torrent of spunk up her bowels, while the Superior at the same moment loaded her womb with his contributions.

Thus surrounded, Bella received the united discharge of the three vigorous priests.

CHAPTER V

Three days after the events detailed in the preceeding pages, Bella made her appearance in her uncle's drawing-room, as rosy and as charming as ever.

My movements in the meantime had been erratic, for my appetite was by no means small, and new features always possessed a certain piquancy for me which prevented too protracted a residence in one locality.

It was thus I found means to overhear a conversation which not a little astonished me; but which, as it bears directly upon the events I am describing, I do not hesitate to disclose.

It was thus I became acquainted with the real depth and subtlety of the character of Father Ambrose.

I am not going to reproduce this discourse here as I heard it from my vantage-ground; it will be sufficient, if I explain the principal ideas if conveyed and relate the application.

It was clear that Ambrose was annoyed and discomfitted at the abrupt participation of his "confreres" in the enjoyment of his latest acquisition, and he concocted a daring and devilish scheme to frustrate their interference, while at the same time appearing himself to be entirely innocent of the business.

In short, with this view, Ambrose went direct to Bella's uncle, and related how he had discovered his niece and her young lover in Cupid's alliance, and how there was no doubt she had received and reciprocated the last tokens of his passion.

In so doing the wily priest had an ulterior object in view. He well knew the character of the man with whom he had to deal. He knew also that sufficient of his own real life was not entirely hidden from the uncle.

In fact, the pair pretty well understood one another. Ambrose had strong passions, and was amatory to an extraordinary extent. So was Bella's uncle.

The latter had confessed as much to Ambrose, and in the course of this confession, had given evidence of such irregular desires as to raise no difficulties in making him a ready participator in the plans which the other had originated.

Mr. Verbouc's eyes had long been cast in secret upon

his niece. He had confessed it. Ambrose brought him suddenly a piece of news which opened his eyes to the fact that she had begun to entertain sentiments of the same sort for others of his sex.

The character of Ambrose occured immediately to him. He was his spiritual confessor; he asked his advice.

The holy man gave him to understand that his chance had come, and that it would be to their mutual advantage to share the prize between them.

This proposition touched a chord in the character of Verbouc of which Ambrose was already not entirely ignorant. If any fact lent greater enjoyment to his sensuality, or gave more poignancy to his indulgences, it was to witness another in the act of complete carnal copulation, and then afterwards to complete his own gratification by a second penetration and emission upon the body of the same patient.

Thus the compact was soon made; an opportunity was found; the necessary privacy secured, for Bella's aunt was an invalid and confined to her room; and then Ambrose prepared Bella for the event about to take place.

After a short preliminary discourse, in which he cautioned her not to say a word of their previous intimacy, and informed her that her relative had somehow discovered her intrigue, he led her round gradually to the fact which he had all along had in view. He even told her of the passion her uncle had conceived for her, and declared, in plain terms, that the surest way to avoid his heavy resentment was to prove obedient to all he might require of her.

Mr. Verbouc was a man of hale and vigorous build, and of about fifty years of age. As her uncle he had always inspired Bella with the greatest respect, in which was mingled not a little awe of his presence and authority. He had treated her since the death of his brother, if not with affection, at least not unkindly, though with a reserve which was natural to his character.

Bella had evidently no reason to hope for any clemency on this occasion, or to expect any escape from her indignant relative.

I pass over the first quarter of an hour, the tears of Bella, and the embarrassment with which she found herself at once the recipient of her uncle's too tender embraces and of his well-deserved carless.

The interesting comedy proceeded little by little, until Mr. Verbouc, taking his pretty niece between his knees, audaciously unfolded the design he had formed of enjoying her himself.

"There must be no silly resistance, Bella," continued her uncle; "I will have no hesitation, no affectation of modesty. It is sufficient that this good Father has sanctified the operation, and I must therefore possess and enjoy your body as your imprudent young companion has already done with your consent."

Bella was utterly confounded. Although sensual, as we have already seen, to an extent not often found in girls of such tender age, she had been brought up in those strict and conventional views which assorted with the severe and repelling character of her relative. All her horror of such a crime at once rose before her. Not even the presence and alleged sanction of Father Ambrose could lessen the distrust with which she viewed the horrible proposal now deliberately made to her.

Bella trembled with surprise and terror at the nature of the crime contemplated. This new position shocked her. The change from the reserved and severe uncle, whose wrath she had always deprecated and feared, and whose precepts she had long accustomed herself to receive with reverence, to the ardent admirer, thirsting for possession of those favours which she had so recently bestowed upon another, struck her dumb with amazement and disgust.

Meanwhile Mr. Verbouc, who was evidently not disposed to allow time for reflection, and whose disorder was plainly visible in more ways than one, took his young niece in his arms, and despite her reluctance, covered her face and neck with forbidden and passionate kisses.

Ambrose, to whom the girl turned in this exigency afforded her no solace, but on the contrary smiling grimly at the other's emotion, encouraged him by secret glances to carry to the last extremity his pleasures and his lubricity.

Resistance, under such trying circumstances, was difficult.

Bella was young and comparatively powerless in the strong grip of her relative. Lashed to frenzy by the contact and obscene touches in which he now indulged himself, Mr. Verbouc sought with redoubled energy to possess himself of the person of his niece. Already his nervous fingers pressed the beautiful satin of her thighs. Another determined push, and in spite of the close pressure which Bella continued to exert in her defence, the lewd hand covered the rosy lips, and the trembling fingers divided the close and moistened chink of modesty's stronghold.

Up to this point Ambrose had remained a quiet observer of this exciting conflict; now, however, he also advanced, and passing his powerful left arm round the young girl's slender waist, seized both her small hands in his right, and having thus pinned her, left her an easy prey to the lascivious approaches of her relative.

"For mercy's sake," moaned Bella, panting with her exertions, "Let me go; it is too horrible—it is monstrous—cruel that you are! I am lost!"

"Nay, my pretty niece, not lost," replied her uncle, "only awakened to those pleasures which Venus has in store for her votaries, and which love reserves for those who are bold enough to seize upon them and enjoy them, while they may."

"I have been horribly deceived." cried Bella, little softened by this ingenious explanation. "I see it all. Oh! shame. I cannot let you, I cannot let you, I cannot. Oh, no! I cannot. Holy Mother! Let me go, Uncle. Oh! oh!"

"Be quiet, Bella; you must indeed submit; I will enjoy you by force, if you do not allow me to do so otherwise. There, open these pretty legs, let me feel these exquisite calves these soft luscious thighs: let me put my hand upon this heaving little belly—nay, hold still, little fool. You are mine at last. Oh, how I have longed for this, Bella!"

Bella, however, still kept up a certain resistance, which only served to whet the unnatural appetite of her assailant, while Ambrose held her firmly in his clutches.

"Oh, the beautiful bottom!" exclaimed Verbouc, as he slipped his intruding hand beneath the velvet thighs of poor Bella, and felt the rounded globes of her charming "derriere". "Ah! the glorious bottom. All is mine now. All shall be feted in good time."

"Let me go," cried Bella. "Oh! oh!"

These last exclamations were wrung from the pretty girl, as between the two man they forced her backwards upon the couth which stood conveniently within reach.

As she fell, she reclined upon the stout body of Ambrose, while Mr. Verbouc, who had now raised her clothes, and lewdly exposed the silk-clad legs and exquisite proportions of his niece, drew back for a moment to enjoy at his ease the indecent exhibition which he had forcibly provided for his own amusement.

"Uncle, are you mad?" cried Bella, once more, as with wriggling limbs, she vainly strove to conceal the luscious nudity now fully exposed. "Pray, let me go."

"Yes, Bella, I am mad—mad with passion for you—mad with lust to possess you, to enjoy you, to satiate myself upon your body. Resistance is useless; I will have my will and revel in those pretty charms, in that tight and exquisite little sheath."

Thus saying, Mr. Verbouc prepared himself for the final act of the incestuous drama. He unfastened his nether garments, and discarding all considerations of modesty, wantonly allowed his niece to behold in full view the plump and rubicund proportions of his excited member, which, erect into glowing, now menaced her directly in front.

A moment later and Verbouc threw himself upon his prey, firmly held down by the recumbent priest; then applying his rampant weapon point blank to the tender orifice he essayed to complete the conjunction by inserting its large and long proportions in the body of his niece.

But the continued writhing of Bella's young form, the disgust and horror which had seized upon her, and the almost immature dimensions of her parts, effectually prevented him from gaining so easy a victory as he desired.

Never had I longed so ardently to contribute to the discomforture of a champion as on the present occasion, and moved by the complaints of the gentle Bella, with the body of a flea and the soul of a wasp, I hopped at one bound to the rescue.

To dig my probocis into the sensitive covering of the scrotum of Mr. Verbouc was the work of a second. It had the desired effect. A sharp and tingling sensation of pain made him pause. The interval was fatal, and the next moment the thighs and stomach of the young Bella were covered with the wasted superfluity of her incestuous relative's vigour.

Curses—not loud, but deep—followed this unexpected contre-temps. The would be ravisher withdraw from his vantage-ground, and unable to continue the conflict, reluctantly put up the discomfited weapon.

No sooner had Mr. Verbouc released his niece from this trying position than Father Ambrose commenced to manifest the violence of his own excitement, produced from his passive observance of the foregoing erotic scene. While still retaining his powerful grasp on Bella, and thus gratifying his sense of touch, the appearance of his dress in front plainly denoted the state of affairs as regarded his readiness to take advantage of the occasion. His redoutable weapon, seemingly disdaining the confinement of his garments, protruded itself into view, the big round head already skinned and throbbing with eagerness for enjoyment.

"Ah!" exclaimed the other, as his lewd glance fell upon the distended weapon of his confessor, "here is a champion, who will brook no defeat, I warrant," and deliberately taking it in his hand, he manipulated the huge shaft with evident satisfaction.

"What a monster! How strong it is—how stiff it stands!"

Father Ambrose rose, his crimson face betrayed the intensity of his desire; placing the frightened Bella in a more propitious attitude, he brought the broad red knob to the moistened aperture, and proceeded to force it inwards with a desperate effort.

Pain, agitation, and longing coursed each other through the nervous system of the young victim of lust,

Although the present was not the first occasion on which the reverend Father had stormed the mosscovered outworks, yet the fact of her uncle's presence, the indelicacy of the whole scene, and the innate conviction, now first dawning upon her, of the trickery and selfishness of the holy man, combined to repel within her those extreme sensations of pleasure which had before so powerfully manifested themselves.

But the proceedings of Ambrose left Bella no time for reflection, for feeling the delicate sheath press glove-like around his large weapon, he hasteded to complete the conjunction, and with a few vigorous and skilful bounds, plunged himself to the balls in her body.

Then followed a rapide interval of fierce enjoyment—of rapid thrusts and pressures, firm and close, until a low, gurgling cry from Bella announced that Nature had asserted herself, and that she had arrived at that exquisite crisis in love's combat, when spasms of unspeakable pleasure pass rapidly, voluptuously through the nerves, and with head thrown back, lips parted, and fingers convulsively working, the whole body rigid with the absorbing effort, the nymph gives down her youthful essence to meet the coming gushes from her lover.

Bella's writhing from, upturned eyes, and clutching hands sufficiently bespoke her condition without the estatic moan which broke laboriously from her quivering lips.

The whole bulk of the potent shaft, now well lubricated, worked deliciously within her young parts. The excitement of Ambrose increased each instant, and his instrument, hard as iron, threatened with each plunge to discharge its reeking essence.

"Oh, I can do no more; I feel my spunk is nearly coming. Verbouc, you must fuck her. She is delicious. Her belly clips me like a glove. Oh! Oh! Ah!"

Stronger, closer thrusts—a vigorous bound—a sinking

of the strong man upon the slight figure of the girl—a hard, low grasp, she Bella, with ineffable delight, felt the hot injection spouting from her ravisher, and pouring in volumes, thick and slippery far within her tender parts.

Ambrose reluctantly withdrew his smoking prick, and left displayed the glistening parts of the young girl, from which trickled a thick mass of his spending.

"Good," exclaimed Verbouc, on whom the scene had had a powerfully exciting effect, "It is now my turn, good Father Ambrose! You have enjoyed my niece under my eyes; that is as I wished, and she has been well ravished. She has also partaken of the pleasure with you; my anticipations are realised; she can receive, she can enjoy; one can satiate oneself with her, and in her body: good—I am going to began. My opportunity has come at last, she cannot escape me now. I am going to satisfy my long cherished desire. I am going to appease this insatiable lust for my brother's child. See this member, how he raises his red head, it is my desire for you, Bella feel, my sweet niece, how hard your dear uncle's balls are—they are filled for you. It is you who have made this thing so stiff, and long, and swollen—it is you who are destined to bring it relief. Skin it back, Bella! So, my child—let me guide your pretty hand. Oh! no nonsense—no blushes—no modesty—no reluctance—do you see its length? You must take it all into that hot little slit that dear Father Ambrose has just so well filled. Do you observe my big globes beneath, Bella daring? They are loaded with the spunk I am going to discharge for your pleasure and my own. Yes, Bella, into the belly of my brother's child."

The idea of the horrid incest he contemplated evidently added fuel to his excitement, and produced within him a surabundant sensation of lustful impatience, which exhibited itself no less in his inflamed countenance than in the stiffened and erected shaft which now menaced Bella's moistened parts.

Mr. Verbouc took his measures securely. There was indeed, as he said, no escape for poor Bella. He mounted upon her body, he opened her legs. Ambrose held her firmly against his belly as he reclined. The ravisher saw his chance, the way was clear, the white thighs already parted, the red and glistening lips of the pretty young cunt confronted him. He could wait longer; parting the lips and pointing aright the dull red head of his weapon to the pouting slit, he now drove forward, and at one bound, with a yell of sensual pleasure, buried himself to his utmost length in his niece's belly.

"Oh, Lord: I'm in her at last," screamed Verbouc. "Oh! ah! What pleasure—how nice she is—how tight. Oh!"

Good Father Ambrose held her fast.

Bella gave a violent start, and a little scream of pain and terror, as she felt the entry of her uncle's swollen member; while, firmly embedded in the warm person of his victim, he commenced a quick and furious career of selfish pleasure. It was the lamb in the clutches of the wolf, the dove in the talons of the eagle—merciless, regardless of her own feelings, the brute bore all before him, until, too soon for his own hot lust, with a scream of agonised enjoyment, he discharged, and shot into his niece a plentiful torrent of his incestuous fluid.

Again and again the two wretches enjoyed their young victim. Their hot lust, stimulated by the prospect of each other's pleasures, drove them to madness.

Ambrose essayed to attack her in the buttocks, but Verbouc, who doubtless had his own reasons for the prohibition, forbade the violation, and the priest, no ways abashed, lowered the knob of his big tool, and drove it up furiously into her little slit from behind. Verbouc knelt below, and watched the act, and at its conclusion sucked, with evident delight, the streaming lips of his young niece's well filled cunt.

That night I accompanied Bella to her couch, for though my nerves had received a dreadful shock, my appetite had suffered no diminution, and it was lucky; perhaps, that my young "protegee" was not possessed of so irritable a skin as to resent to any great extent my endeavous to satisfy my natural cravings.

Sleep had succeeded the repast with which I had regaled myself, and I had found deliciously warm and secure retreat amid the soft and tender moss which covered the mount of the fair Bella when, at about midnight, a violent disturbances roughly roused me from my dignified repose.

A rude and powerful grasp was upon the young girl, and a heavy form pressed vigorously upon her little figure. A stifled cry came from her frightened lips, and amid vain struggles on her part to escape and more successful efforts to prevent that desirable consummation on the part of her assailant, I recognised the voice and person of Mr. Verbouc.

The surprise had been complete; vain was all the feeble resistance that his niece could offen, as with feverish haste, and dreadfully excited by the soft contact of her velvet limbs, the incestuous uncle fiercely possessed himself of her most secret charms, and strong in his hideous lust, drove his rampant weapon into her young body.

Then followed a struggle in which both played a distinct part.

The revisher, fired equally by the difficulties of his conquest, as well as by the exquisite sensations he was enjoying, buried his stiff member in the luscious sheath, and sought by his fervid thrusts to ease his lust in a copious discharge, while Bella, whose prudent temperament was not proof against so strong and lascivious an attack, strove in vain to resist the violent efforts of nature, which, roused by the exciting friction, threatened to turn traitor, until at length with quiverings limbs and gasping breath, she surrendered and gave down the sweet outpourings of her inmost soul upon the swollen shaft which so deliciously throbbed within her.

Mr. Verbouc was fully aware of his advantage and changing his tactics, like a prudent general, he took care not to expend all his own climax and provoked a fresh advance on the part of his gentle combatant.

Mr. Verbouc had not great difficulty in the matter, and the conflict appeared to excite him to fury. The bed trembled and shook, the whole room vibrated with the tremulous energy of his lascivious attack, the two bodies heaved rolled, plunged in an undistinguishable mass.

Lust, hot and impatient, reigned paramount on both sides. He lunged—he strove—he pushed—he thrust—he drew back until the broad red head of his swollen penis lay between the rosy lips of Bella's hot parts. He drove forward until the crisp black hairs of his belly mingled with the soft mossy down which covered the plump mount of his niece, until, with a quivering sob, she expressed at once her pain and her pleasure.

Once more the victory was his, and as his vigorous member sheathed itself to the hilt in her soft person, a low, tender, wailing cry bespoke her ecstasy as once more the keen spasm of pleasure broke over her nervous system; and then, with a groam of brutal triumph, he shot a hot stream of trickling fluid into the furthest recesses of her womb.

Endowed with the frenzy of newly-awakened desire, and still unsatisfied with the possession of so fair a flower, the brutal Verbouc next turned his half fainting niece upon her face, and contemplated at his ease her lovely buttocks. His object became evident, as procuring some of the spendings with which her little slit was now loaded, he annointed her anus, pushing his forefinger therein as far as it would go.

His passions were again at fever point. His prick menaced her plump bottom, and turning upon her recumbent body, he placed the shining knob to the tight little aperture, and endeavoured to ram it in. In this, after a time, he succeeded, and Bella received in her rectum the entire length of her uncle's yard. The tightness of her anus afforded him the most poignant pleasure, and he continued to work slowly up and down for at least a quarter of an hour, at the end of which time his prick became hard as iron, and the child felt him squirting hot floods of spunk into bowels.

It was daylight before Mr. Verbouc released his niece from the lustful embraces in which he had satiated his passion, and then slunk weakly away to his own cold couch; while, worn and jaded. Bella sank into a deep slumber of exhaustion, from which she did not awake until a late hour.

When next Bella emerged from her chamber, it was with a sense of change in herself which she neither cared nor sought to analyse. Passion had asserted itself in her character; strong sexual emotions had been awakened, and had also been gratified. Refinement of indulgence had generated lust, and lust had rendered easy the road to unrestrained and even unnatural gratification.

Bella, young, child-like, and so lately innocent, had suddenly become a woman of violent passions and unrestrained lust.

CHAPTER VI

I shall not trouble the reader with the conditions under which one day I found myself snugly concealed upon the person of good Father Clement, or pause here to explain how it was I was present when that worthy ecclesiastic received and confessed a very charming and stylish young lady of some twenty years of ago.

I soon discovered from their subsequent conversation

that the lady was not of titled rank, though closely connected, but married to one of the wealthiest landed proprietors in the neighbourhood.

Names are of no importance here. I, therefore, suppress that of this fair penitent.

After the confessor had ended his benediction, and had concluded the ceremony by which he became the depository of the lady's choicest secrets, he led her, nothing loath, from the body of the church into the same small sacristy where Bella had received her lesson in sanctified copulation.

The door was bolted, no time was lost, the lady dropped her robe, the stalwart confessor opened his cassock, disclosing his enormous weapon, the ruby head of which now stood distended and threatening in the air. The lady no sooner perceived this apparition, than she seized upon it with the air of one to whom it was by no means a new object of delight.

Her dainty hand stroked gently the upright pillar of hard muscle and her eyes devoured its long and swollen proportions.

"You shall do it to me from behind," remarked the lady—"en levrette, but you must be very careful; you are so fearfally large."

Father Clement's eyes glistened under his large head of red hair, and his big weapon gave a spasmodic throb that would have lifted a chair.

In another second the young lady had placed herself on her knees upon the seat, and Clement coming close behind her, lifted up her fine white linen, and exposed a plump and well-rounded bottom beneath which, half hidden by the swelling thighs, were just visible the red lips of a delicious slit, luxuriantly shaded with the ample growth of rich brown hair which curled about it.

Clement wanted no further incitement; spitting on the knob of his great member, he pushed its warm head in between the moist lips, and then with many heaves, and much exertion, he strove to make it enter to the balls.

He went in—and in—and in, until it seemed as though the fair recipient could not possibly stow away any more without danger to her vitals. Meanwhile her face betrayed the extraordinary emotion the gigantic ram was occasioning her.

Presently Father Clement stopped. He was in up to his balls. His red crispy hair pressed the plump cheeks of the lady's bottom. She had received the entire length of his yard in her body. Then began an encounter which fairly shook the bench and all the furniture in the room.

Passing his arms around the fair form in his clutches, the sensual priest pressed himself inwards at every thrust, only withdrawing one half his length the better to force it home, until the lady quivered again with the exquisite sensations so vigorous a stretching was affording her. Then her eyes closed, her head fell forward, and she poured down upon the invader a warm gush of nature's essence.

Meanwhile Father Clement worked away in the hot sheath, each moment only serving to render his thick weapon harder and stronger until it resembled nothing so much as a bar of solid iron.

But all things have an end, and so had the enjoyment of the good priest, for having pushed and strove, and pressed and battered with his furious yard until he too could hold back no longer, he felt himself upon the point of discharging his metal, and thus bringing matters to a climax.

It came at last, as with a sharp cry of ecstasy he sank forward upon the body of the lady, his member buried to the roots in her belly, and pouring a prolific flood of spunk into her very womb. Presently all was over, the last spasm had passed, the last reeking drop had issued, and Clement lay still as death.

The reader must not imagine that good Father Clement was satisfied with the single "coup" which he had just delivered with such excellent effect; or that the lady, whose wanton sympathies had been so powerfully assuaged, desired to abstain from all further dalliance. On the contrary, this act of copulation had only roused the dormant faculties of sensuality in both, and again they now sought to allay the burning flame of lust.

The lady fell on her back; her burly ravisher threw himself upon her, and driving in his battering ram until their hairs met, he spent again and filled her womb with a viscid torrent.

Still unsatisfied, the wanton pair continued their exciting pastime.

This time Clement lay upon his back, and the lady lasciviously toying with his huge genitals, took the thick red head of his penis between her rosy lips, and after stimulating him to the utmost tension by her maddening touches greedily induced a discharge of his prolific fluid, which, thick and warm, now spouted into her pretty mouth and down her throat.

Then the lady, whose wantonness at least equalled that of her coufessor, stood across his muscular from, and after having secured another determined and enormous erection, lowered herself upon the throbbing shaft, impaled her beautiful figure upon the mass of flesh and muscle until nought was left to view save the big balls which hung close below the stiffened weapon. Thus she pumped from Clement a fourth discharge, and reeking in the excessive outpouring of the seminal fluid, as well as fatigued with the unusual duration of the pastime she disappeared to contemplate at leisure the monstrous proportions and unusual capabilities of her gigantic confessor.

CHAPTER VII

Bella had a female friend, a young lady, a few months older than herself, and the daughter of a wealthy gentleman who lived very near Mr. Verbouc. Julia was, however, of a less voluptuous and ardent disposition, and, Bella soon found, was not ripe enough to comprehend the sentiments of passion nor understand the strong instincts which provoke to enjoyment.

Julia was slightly taller than her young friend, slightly less plump, but formed to delight the eye and ravish the heart of an artist by her faultless shape and exquisite features.

A flea cannot well be supposed to describe personal beauty, even in those on whom they feed. All I know is that Julia was a luscious treat to me, and would one day also be to some one of the opposite sex, for she was made to raise the desires of the most callous, and to charm by her graceful manners and ever pleasing shape the most fastidious votaries of Venus.

Julia's father possessed, as we have said, ample means; her mother was a weak simpleton, who busied herself very little about her daughter, or, indeed, anything beyond the religious duties in the exercise of which she spent a great part of her time, or the visitations of the old "devotes" of the neighbourhood, who encouraged her predilections.

Monsieur Delmont was comparatively young. He was robust, he was fond of life, and as his pious better half was far too much occupied to afford him those matrimonial solaces which the poor man had a right to expect he went elsewhere.

M. Delmont had a mistress—a young and pretty woman, who I concluded was, in her turn, indisposed after the fashion of such people, to be content only with her wealthy protector.

M. Delmont by no means confined his attentions even to his mistress; his habits were erratic, and his tastes decidedly amatory.

Under these circumstances it was not wonderful that his eye should have fallen upon the budding and beautiful figure of his daughter's young friend, Bella. Already he had found opportunities to press the pretty gloved hand, to kiss—of course in a properly paternal manner—the white brow and even to place his trembling hand—quite by accident—upon the plump thighs.

In fact, Bella, wiser far and more experienced than most girls of her tender age, saw that he was only awaiting an opportunity to push matters to extremities.

This was just what Bella would have liked, but she was too closely watched, and the new and disgraceful connection in which she was only just entering occupied all her thoughts.

Father Ambrose, however, was fully alive to the necessity of caution, and the good man let no opportunity pass by, while the young lady was in his confessional, of making direct and pertinent enquiries as to her conduct with others and theirs to his penitent. It was thus Bella came to confess to her spiritual guide the feelings engendered within herself by the amatory proceedings of M. Delmont.

Father Ambrose gave her some good advice, and immediately set Bella to work to suck his penis.

This delicious episode over, and the traces of his enjoyment removed, the worthy man set about with his usual astuteness, to turn the fact he had just acquired to his advantage.

Nor was it long before his sensual and vicious brain conceived a plot which for criminality and audacity I, as a humble insect, have never known equalled.

Of course he had at once determined that the young Julia should eventually be his—that was only natural—but to accomplish this end and amuse himself at the same time with the passion which M. Delmont evidently entertained for Bella, was a double consummation which he saw his way to by a most unscrupulous and hideous plan, which the reader will understand as we proceed.

The first thing to be done was to warm the imagination of the fair Julia, and develop in her the latent fires of lust.

This noble task the good priest left to Bella who, duly instructed, easily promised compliance.

Since the ice had been broken in her own case, Bella to say the truth, desired nothing better than to make Julia equally culpable as herself. So Bella set to work to corrupt her young friend. How she succeeded, we shall duly see.

It was only a few days after the initiation of the young Bella into the delights of crime in the shape of incest, which we have already related, and the little girl had no further experience, Mr. Verbouc having been called away from home. At length, however, an opportunity occurred, and for the second time Bella found herself alone and serene with her uncle and Father Ambrose.

The evening was cold, but a pleasant warmth was imparted to the luxurious apartment by a stove, while the soft and elastic sofa and ottomans with which the room was furnished gave an air of listless repose. In the brilliant light of a deliciously perfumed lamp, the two men appeared like the luxurious votaries of Bacchus and Venus, as they reclined only lightly clad, and fresh from a somptuous repast.

As for Bella, she surpassed herself in beauty. Habited in a charming "neglige," she half disclosed and half concealed those budding sweets of which she might well be proud.

The lovely rounded arms, the soft, silk-clad legs, the heaving bosom, whence peeped two white, exquisitely formed and strawberry-tipped "pommettes," the well-turned ankle, and the tiny foot, cased in its close-fitting little shoe: These and other beauties lent their several attractions to make up a delicate and delicious whole, with which the pampered Detities might have intoxicated themselves, and in which two lustful mortals now prepared to revel.

It needed little, however, to excite further the infamous and irregular desires of the two men, who now, with eyes red with lust, regarded at their ease the luxurious treat in store for them.

Secure from all interruption, both sought in lascivious "attouchments" to gratify the craving of their imaginations to handle what they saw.

Unable to restrain his eagerness, the sensual uncle stretched out his hand, and drawing his beautiful niece close to him, allowed his fingers to wander between her legs. As for the priest he seized on her soft bosom, and buried his face in its young freshness.

Neither allowed any considerations of modesty to interfere in their enjoyments, and the members of the two strong men were fully exposed and standing excitingly erect, the red heads shining with the tension of blood and muscle below.

"Oh, how you touch me," murmured Bella, opening involuntarily her white thighs to the trembling hand of her uncle, while Ambrose almost stifled her with his gross lips, as he sucked delicious kisses from her ruby mouth.

Presently her delighted hand pressed within its warm palm the stiffened member of the vigorous Priest.

"There, my sweet girl, is it not large? And does it not burn to spout its juices into you? Oh, my child, how you excite me. Your hand, your little hand! Ugh! I am dying to thrust this into your soft belly! Kiss me, Bella! Verbouc, see how your niece excites me."

"Holy Mother, what a prick! See, what a nut it has,

Bella. How it shines, what a long white shaft, and how it curves upwards, like a serpent bent on stinging its victim. Already a drop gathers on its tip, look, Bella.''

"Oh, how hard it is! How it throbs! How it thrusts forward! I can scarce hold it, you kill me with such kisses, you suck my life away."

Mr. Verbouc made a forward movement, and at the same moment again disclosed his weapon, erect and ruby red, the head uncapped and moist.

Bella's eyes glistened at the prospect.

"We must regulate our pleasures, Bella," said her Uncle. "We must endeavour, as much as possible, to prolong our ecstasies."

"Ambrose is rampant with lust, what a splendid animal he is, what a member; he is furnished like a jackass. Ah, my niece, my child, that will stretch your little slit, it will thrust itself right up to your vitals, and after a long course it will discharge a forrent of spunk for your pleasure."

"What joy," murmured Bella; "I long to have it up me to the waist."

"Yes, oh yes; do not hasten too soon the delicious end; let us all work for that."

She would have added more, but the red bulb of Mr. Verbouc's stiffened affair at that moment entered her mouth.

With the utmost avidity Bella received the stiff and throbbing thing between her coral lips, and allowed as much of the head and shoulders as could accommodate themselves to enter. She licked at round with her tongue; she even tried to force the tip into the red opening at the apex. She was excited beyond herself. Her cheeks flushed, her breath came and went with spasmodic eagerness. Her hand still grasped the member of the salacious Priest. Her tight young cunt throbbed with the pleasures of anticipation.

She would have continued to tickle, rub, and excite the swollen tool of the lecherous Ambrose, but that worthy man signed to her to stop.

"Stay a moment, Bella," sighed he, "you will make the spunk come so."

Bella released her hold of the big white shaft and lay back, so that her Uncle could work leisurely in and out of her mouth Her eyes greedily rested upon the huge proportions of Ambrose all the while.

Never had Bella tasted a prick with so much delight, as she now did the very respectable weapon of her Uncle. She, therefore, worked her lips upon it with the utmost relish, sucking greedily the moisture which from time to time exuded from the tip. Mr. Verbouc was in raptures with her willing services.

The Priest now knelt down, and pushing his shaven head between the knees of Mr. Verbouc, as he stood before his niece, he opened the girl's plump thighs, and parting the pink lips of her delicate slit with his fingers, he thrust in his tongue, and covered her young and excited parts with his thick lips.

Bella shivered with pleasure: her Uncle grew stiffer, and pushed hard and viciously at her beautiful mouth. The girl placed a hand on his balls, and gently squeezed them. She skinned back the hot shaft and sucked it with evident delight.

"Let it come," said Bella, rejecting for a moment the glistening nut in order to express herself and take breath. "Let it come, Uncle, I should like to taste it so much."

"So you shall, my darling, but not yet, we must not be too quick,"

"Oh! How he sucks me, how his tongue licks me! I am on fire; he is killing me."

95

"Aha, Bella, you feel nothing but pleasures now, you are reconciled to the joys of our incestuous connection."

"Indeed I am, my dear Uncle, give me your prick again in my mouth."

"Not yet, Bella, my love."

"Do not keep me too long. You are maddening me. Father! Father! Oh, he is coming to me, he is preparing to fuck me. Holy mother! What a prick! Oh, mercy! He will split me."

Meanwhile Ambrose, driven to fury by the delicious employment he had been engaged in, became too excited to remain longer as he was, and taking the opportunity of Mr. Verbouc's temporary withdrawal, he rose and pushed the beautiful girl back upon the soft lounge.

Verbouc seized upon the formidable penis of the holy Father, and gave it one or two preliminary shakes, pushed back the soft skin which circled the egg-shaped head, and directing the broad flaming head to the pink slit, drove it up vigorously into her belly, as she lay before him.

The moistened condition of he child's parts assisted the insertion of the head and shoulders, and the Priest's weapon was quickly engulphed. Vigorous thrusts succeeded, and with fierce lust in his face, and little mercy for the youth of his victim, Ambrose fucked on. Her excitement obliterated all sense of pain and stretching wide her pretty legs she allowed him to wallow as completely as he desired in the possession of her beauty.

A loud moan of rapture escaped from Bella's parted lips, as she felt the huge weapon, hard as iron, pressing up her womb, and stretching her with its great bulk.

Mr. Verbouc lost nothing of the salacious sight, but standing close to the excited couple, he placed his own hardly less vigorous member in his niece's convulsive grasp.

Ambrose no sooner felt himself securely lodged in the beautiful body beneath him than he curbed his eagerness, and calling to his aid the wonderful power of self-control which he possessed in so extraordinary a degree, he passed his trembling hands behind the hips of the girl, and pulling apart his dress exposed his hairy belly, with which at each deep thrust he rubbed her soft "motte".

But now the Priest commenced his course in earnest. With strong and regular thrusts he buried himself in the tender form beneath him. He pressed hotly forward; Bella threw her white arms round his brawny neck. His balls beat upon her plump bottom, his tool was up her to the hairs, which, black and crisp, plentifully covered his big belly.

"She has it now; look, Verbouc, at your niece. See, how she relishes the administrations of the church. Ah, what pressures! How she nips me in her tight, naked little cunt."

"Oh, my dear, dear. Oh! good Father, fuck on, I am spending; push, push it in. Kill me with it, if you like, but keep moving. So! Oh! Heavens. Ah! Ah! How big it is; how you enter me!"

The lounge fairly worked again, and cracked beneath his rapid strokes.

"Oh, God!" cried Bella "he's killing me—it's really to muuh—I die—I am spending," and with a half shriek, the girl went off and flooded the thick member which was so deliciously forging her—a second time.

The long prick grew hotter and harder. The knob swelled also, and the whole tremendous affair seemed ready to burst with luxury. The young Bella moaned incoherent words, in which the word fuck was alone audible.

Ambrose, also fully prime, and felling his great affair nipped in the young parts of the girl, could hold out no longer, and catching hold of Bella's bottom with both hands, he pressed inwards the whole tremendous length and discharged, shooting the thick jets of his fluid, one after another, deep into his play-fellow.

A roar like that of a wild beast escaped him, as he felt the hot spunk spout from him.

"Oh! it comes; you are flooding me. I feel it. Oh! delicious!"

Meanwhile the Priest's prick bore hard up into Bella's body, and its swollen head continued to inject its pearly seed right into her young womb.

"Oh, what a quantity you have given me," remarked Bella, as she staggered to her feet and beheld the thick, hot fluid running in all directions down her legs. "How white and slippery it is."

This was exactly the condition of affairs which Uncle most coveted, and he, therefore proceeded leisurely to avail himself of it. He regarded her beautiful silk stockings all drabbled; he pushed his fingers between the red lips of her young cunt and rubbed the exuding semen all over her hairless young belly and thighs.

Placing his niece conveniently before him, Mr. Verbouc exposed once more his stiff and hairy champion, and roused by the exceptional circumstances he so much delighted in, he contemplated with eager zeal the tender parts of the young Bella, all covered as they were with the discharge of the Priest, and still exuding thick and copious gouttes of his prolific fluid.

Bella, at his desire, opened her legs to her utmost. Her

uncle eagerly pushed his naked person between her plump young thighs.

"Hold still, my dear niece. My prick is not so thick, nor so long as Father Ambrose's, but I know well how to fuck, and you shall try whether your Uncle's spunk is not as thick and pungent as any ecclesiastic's. See, how stiff I am."

"Ah! how you make me long," said Bella, "I can see your dear thing waiting for its turn; how red it looks. Push me, Uncle, dear, I am ready again, and good Father Ambrose has plentifully oiled the way for you.

The hard and red-headed member touched the parted lips, all slippery as they were already, the spex readily enters—the big shaft quickly follows, and with a few steady thrusts, behold this exemplary relative buried to the balls in his niece's belly, and lolling luxuriantly in the reeking evidence of her previous unholy enjoyment of Father Ambrose.

"My darling Uncle," exclaimed the girl, "remember whom you fuck. It is no stranger, it is your brother's child—your own niece. Fuck me then. Uncle, give me all your strong prick—fuck! Ah, fuck, fuck, till your incestuous stuff pours into me. Ah, ah! Oh!!" and overpowered with the salacious ideas she conjured up, Bella gave way to the most unbridled sensuality, to the great delight of her Uncle.

The strong man, content in the gratification of his favourite lechery, deals his rapid and powerful strokes. Swimming as was the condition of his fair oppenent's slit, it was so naturally small and tight and he found himself clipped in the most delicious way by the narrow opening, and his pleasure rapidly advanced.

Verbouc rose and fell upon the delicious body of his

young niece; he drove fiercely inwards at every bound, and Bella clung to him with the tenacity of yet unsated lust. His prick grew hard and hot.

The titillation soon became almost insupportable. Bella herself enjoyed the incestuous encounter to the utmost, until with a sob Mr. Verbouc fell forward spending upon his niece, while the hot fluid spouted from him, and again inundated her womb. Bella also reached the climax and while she felt and welcomed the powerful injection, gave down as equally ardent proof her enjoyment.

The act being thus completed, Bella was permitted to make the necessary ablutions, and then after a revivying glass of wine round, the three sat down, and concerted a devilish plot for the defilment and enjoyment of the beautiful Julia Delmont.

Bella avowed that Mr. Delmont was certainly amorous of her, and evidently only wanted an opportunity to push matters on towards his object.

Father Ambrose confessed that his member stood straight out at the bare mention of the fair girl's name. He confessed her, and he now laughindly acknowledged that he could not keep his hands off himself during the ceremony; her breath caused him agonies of sensual longing, it was perfume itself.

Mr. Verbouc declared himself equally anxious to revel in such tender sweets of which the description made him wild with lust, but how to carry the plot into execution was the question.

"If I ravished her without preparation, I should burst her parts," exclaimed Father Ambrose, displaying once more his rubiconed machine, smoking yet with the unremoved evidence of his last enjoyment.

"I could not have her first. I need the excitement of a previous copulation," objected Mr. Verbouc.

"I should like to see the girl well ravished," said Bella. "I should watch the operation with delight and when Father Ambrose has rammed his big thing into her, you, Uncle, could be giving me yours to compensate me for the gift we were making in favour of the pretty Julia."

"Yes, that would be doubly delicious."

"What is to be done," exclaimed Bella. "Holy Mother! how stiff your thing is again, dear Father Ambrose."

"An idea occurs to me which gives me a violent erection only to think of; put in practice it would be the acme of lust, and consequently of pleasure."

"Let us hear," exclaimed both at once.

"Wait a moment," said the holy man, suffering Bella lightly to skin down the purple head of his tool and tickle the moist orifice with the tip of her tongue.

"Listen to me," said Ambrose. "Mr. Delmont is amorous of Bella there. We are amorous of his daughter, and our child here, who is now sucking my weapon, would like the tender Julia to have it thrust up to her vitals, just by way of giving her wicked salacious little self an extra dose of pleasure. So far we are all agreed. Now give me your attention, and for the moment, Bella, let go my tool. This is my plan. I know the little Julia is not insensible to her animal instincts—in fact, the little devil already feels the pricking of the flesh. A little persuasion and little mystification would do the rest. Julia will consent to have relief from those gentle pangs of canal appetite. Bella must bring her on and encourage the idea. Meanwhile Bella can lead the dear Mr. Delmont further on. She may allow him to declare himself, if he will; in fact this is necessary to the success of the plot; I must than be called in; I will suggest that Mr. Verbouc is a man above all vulgar prejudices, and that for a certain sum to be agreed upon he will surrender his beautiful and virgin niece to his impassionned embraces.''

''I hardly know about that,'' commenced Bella.

''I don't see the object,'' interposed Mr. Verbouc. ''We shall be no nearer the attainment of our aim.''

''Wait a moment,'' continued the holy man. ''We are all agreed so far—now, Bella shall be sold to Mr. Delmont; he shall be allowed to take his full of her beautiful charms in secrecy, she shall not see him, nor he her—at least, not her countenance, which shall remain concealed. He will be introduced to his agreable chamber, he will behold the body, utterly nude, of a lovely young girl, he will know it is his victim, and he will enjoy her.''

''Me!'' interrupted Bella,'' why all this mystery?''

Father Ambrose smiled a sickly smile.

''You will see, Bella—be patient. We want to enjoy Julia Delmont. Mr. Delmont wants to enjoy you. We can only accomplish our purpose by preventing any scandal at the same time. Mr. Delmont must be silenced, or we may suffer for our violation of his child. Now my design is that the lascivious Mr. Delmont shall violate ''his own daughter'' in lieu of Bella, and that having thus opened the way for us, we shall avail ourselves of the fact to satisfy our lust also. If Mr. Delmont falls into the trap, we can either allow him the knowledge of his incest and reward him with the real enjoyment of our sweet Bella, in return for the person of his daughter, or otherwise act as circumstances may dictate.''

''Oh! I am nearly spending,'' cried Mr. Verbouc; ''my weapon is bursting! What a trick! What a delicious sight,''

Both men rose—Bella was enveloped in their embraces—

two hard and large weapons pressed against her soft figure. They led her to the couch.

Ambrose fell upon his back; Bella mounted upon his body, took his stallion penis in her fair hand, and pushed it into her slit.

Mr. Verbouc looked on.

Bella lowered herself down, until the huge weapon was wholly lodged. Then she lay down on the burly Father and commenced an undulating, delicious series of movements.

Mr. Verbouc saw her beautiful bottom rising and falling— parfing and closing with each successive thrust.

Ambrose was in to the hilt, that was evident, his big balls hung closely underneath, and the fat lips of her budding parts came down to them each time she let herself fall above him.

The sight proved too much for him. The virtuous uncle mounted the couch, directed his long and swollen penis to the posteriors of the fair Bella, and with little difficulty succeeded in housing its extreme length in her bowels.

His niece's bottom was broad and soft as velvet, and the skin white as alabaster. Verbouc, however, did not care to stop for contemplation. His member was in, and he felt the tight compression of the muscle at the little entrance acting upon it like nothing else in the world. The two pricks rubbed together with only a thin membrane between.

Bella felt the maddening effect of this double "jouissance". Terrific grew the excitement, until at length the very rapture of the struggle brought its own relief and floods of spunk inundated the fair Bella.

After this, Ambrose discharged twice in Bella's mouth, where uncle also emitted his incestuous fluid, and this final closed the entertainment.

The way in which Bella performed this operation was

such as to call forth the warmest encomiums from her companions.

Seating herself upon the edge of a chair, she received them standing in front of her, so that their stiff weapons were nearly on a level with her coral lips. Then taking the velvet gland entirely into her mouth, she employed her fair hands to rub, tickle, and excite the shaft and its appendages. Thus the full nervous power of her playfellow was employed and with his bursting penis at full stretch, he enjoyed the luscious titillation, until Bella's indelicate touches proved too much, and amid sighs of ecstatic emotion, her mouth and gullet were suddenly flooded with a spouting stream of spunk.

The little glutton swallowed all; she would have done the same for a dozen, had she had the chance.

CHAPTER VIII

Bella continued to afford me the most delicious of pastures. Her young limbs never missed the crimson draughts which I imbibed, or felt, to any grave inconvenience, the tiny punctures which I was forced most reluctantly to make to obtain my living. I determined, therefore, to remain with her although of late her conduct had become, to say the very least, somewhat questionable, and slightly irregular.

One thing I remarked for certain, and that was that she had lost all feelings of delicacy and maidenly reserve, and lived only now for the delights of sensual gratification.

I was soon satisfied that my young lady had lost nothing of the lesson she had received of her share in the conspiracy in course of proparation. How she played her part I now propose to relate.

It was not long before Bella found herself within the mansion of Mr. Delmont, and, as luck would have it, or shall we say rather as that worthy man himself had expressly designed it, alone with the amatory proprietor.

Mr. Delmont saw his chance, and like a clever general instantly pressed on to the assault. He found his fair companion either wholly innocent of his intention, or else wonderfully willing to encourage his advances.

Already Mr. Delmont had his arm around Bella's waist, while apparently, quite by accident, her soft right hand pressed beneath his nervous palm, lay upon his manly thigh.

What Bella felt beneath showed plainly enough the violence of his emotion. A throb passed quickly through the hard object which lay concealed, and Bella was not without the sympathetic spasm that told of sensuous pleasure.

Gently the amorous Mr. D. drew the girl towards him, and hugged her yielding form. He printed sudden a hot kiss on her cheek, and whispered flattering words to adsorb her attention from his proceedings. He essayed more, he gently moved Bella's hand about the hard object, until the young lady perceived that his excitement was likely to become too rapid.

Throughout Bella had firmly adhered to her "role"; she was coy innocence itself.

Mr. D., encouraged by the non-resistance of his young

friend, proceeded to other and still more decided steps. His wanton hand roved along the edge of Bella's light dress, and pressed her yielding calf. Then, suddenly with a warm and simultaneous kiss on her red lips. he quickly passed his trembling fingers underneath and touched her plump thigh.

Bella recoiled. At any other time she would have gladly flung herself upon her back, and bade him do his worst; but she remembered her lesson, and went on with part to perfection.

"Oh! how rude you are," cried the young lady, "what a naughty thing—I cannot let you do that. Uncle says nobody must be allowed to touch that—at any rate not without first——" Bella hesitated, stopped, and looked silly.

Mr. Delmont was curious as well as amatory.

"Without first what, Bella?"

"Oh, I must not tell you. I ought to have said nothing about it; only you, by doing such a rude thing, made me forget."

"Forget what?"

"Something that my Uncle has often told me," answered Bella simply.

"What is it? Tell me."

"I dare not—besides, I do not understand what he means."

"I will explain it, if you tell me what it was he said."

"You promise not to tell?"

"Certainly."

"Well, then, he says I must never let anyone put the hands there, and that whoever wants to do so, must pay well for it."

"Does he really say that?"

"Yes, indeed he does; he says that I am able to bring him a good round sum in that way, and that there are plenty of rich gentlemen who would pay for that you want to do to me, and he says he is not stupid as to lose such a chance."

"Really, Bella, your Uncle is a strict man of business. I did not think he was that kind of man."

"Oh, yes, but he is," cried Bella. "He is very found of money, you know, in secret; and I know scarcely what he means, but he sometimes says he shall sell my maidenhead."

"It is possible," thought Mr. Delmont.

"What a man he must be, what a wonderful eye to business he must have."

In fact, the more Mr. D. thought about it, the more convinced he became of the truth of Bella's ingenious explanation. She was to be bought. He would buy her; better far that way than to run the risk of discovery and punishment by resorting to a secret liaison.

Before, however, he could do more than revolve these sage reflections in his own mind, an interruption occured in the arrival of his own daughter Julia, and very reluctantly he had to release his companion and arrange himself with an eye to propriety.

Bella made a rapid excuse and went home, leaving the event to take its chance.

The route taken by my fair young lady lay through several meadows, and along a cartline which emerged into the great high way very near her Uncle's residence.

The time was afternoon, and the day was unusually fine. The lane had several sudden turnings, and as Bella pursued her way, she amused herself watching the cattle in the neighbouring pastures.

Presently the lane became bordered with trees, the long

straight line of trunks divided the roadway from the footpath. Across the nearest meadow she saw several men at work tilling the ground, and at a little distance, a group of women had ceased for a moment from their labour of weeding to interchange some interesting ideas.

On the opposite side of the lane was a hedge, and looking through this Bella saw a sight which fairly startled her. Within the meadow were two animals, a horse and a mare. The former had evidently been occupied in chasing the latter about the ground, and had at last pinned his compaion in a corner not far from where she stood.

But what startled and surprised Bella most was the wonderful erectioned excitement of a long and grizzly member which hung below the belly of the stallion, and ever and anon sprung up with an impatient jerk against his body.

The mare had evidently remarked it too, for she now stood perfectly quiet with her back towards the horse.

The latter was too pressed by his amorous instincts to dally long beside her, and to the young lady's wonder she beheld the great creature mount up behind the mare and attemp to push his tool into her.

Bella watched with breathless interest, and saw the long swollen member of the horse at length hit the mark and disappear entirely in the hinder parts of the mare.

To say that her sensual feelings were roused would be but to express the natural result of so salacious an exhibition. She was more than roused; her libidinous instincts were "fired". She clutched her hands and gazed with interest on the lewd encounter; and when after a rapid and furious course, the animal withdrew his dripping penis, Bella glared upon it with an insane longing to seize it for herself, and handle the great pendant thing for her own gratification.

In this excited frame of mind, she found that some sort of action was necessary to relieve her from the powerful influence which oppressed her. Making a strong effort, Bella turned her head, and at the same moment, taking half a dozen steps forward, came straight upon a sight which certainly had no tendency to allay her excitement.

Right in her path stood a rustic youth of some eighteen years; his handsome but somewhat stupid features were turned towards the meadow where the amorous steeds were disporting themselves. A gap in the back which bordered the roadway afforded him an excellent view, in the contemplation of which he was evidently as much interested as Bella had been.

But what chained the attention of the girl was the state of the lad's clothing, and the appearence of a tremendous member, rudy and well developed, which, barefaced, and fully exposed, unblushingly raised its fiery crest full in his front.

There was no mistaking the effect the sight in the meadow had produced, for the lad had already unbuttoned his nether garments of coarse material, and had his nervous grasp upon a weapon of which a Carmelite might have been proud. With eager eyes he devoured the scene enacted before him in the meadow, while his right hand skinned the standing column and worked it vigorously up and down, utterly unconscious that so congenial a spirit was witnessing his proceedings.

A start and an exclamation which involuntarily broke from Bella caused him at once to look round, and there, in full view before him stood the beautiful girl, while his nudity and his lewd erection were at the same moment completely exposed.

"Oh, my goodness!" exclaimed Bella, as soon as she could find words, "what a dreadful sight! What a wicked boy; Why, what are you doing with that long red thing?"

The boy, abashed, attempted awkwardly to replace in his breeches the object which had provoked the observations, but his evident confusion and the stiffness of the thing itself rendered the operation very difficult, not to say tedious.

Bella came kindly to the rescue.

"What is that? Let me help you—how came it out? How large and stiff it is, what a length it is! My word! what a tremendously big one you've got; you naughty boy—!"

Suiting the action to the word, the young lady laid her delicate little white hand upon the standing penis of the boy, and squeezing it in her soft warm grasp only, of course, made it the more unlikely to re-enter its retreat.

Meanwhile the lad, gradually recovering his stolid presence of mind, and beholding how fair and apparently innocent was his new acquaintance, ceased to betray any desire to assist her in the laudable endeavors to conceal the stiff and offending member. Indeed, it became impossible, even if he had desired it; for no sooner had her grasp closed upon it, than it acquired even larger proportions, while the distended and purple head shone like a ripe plum.

"What a naughty boy!" observed Bella; "whatever shall I do," she continued, looking archly in the handsome face of the rustic.

"Ah, how nice that is," sighed the lad—"who could

have thought that you were so near me, when I felt so bad, and it first began to throb and swell so just now.''

"This is very, very wicked," remarked the young lady, tightening her grasp, and feeling the rankling flames of lust rising higher and higher within her; "this is dreadfully wrong and naughty, you know it is, you bad boy.''

"Did you see what those horses were doing in the meadow?" asked the boy, looking wonderingly at Bella, whose beauty seemed to dawn upon his dull mind, as the sun steals over a showery landscape.

"Yes, I did," replied the girl, innocently, "what were they doing it for—what did it mean?"

"It means fucking," responded the youth, with a lewd grin. "He wanted the mare, and mare wanted the stallion, and so they came together and fucked.''

"Lord, how curious!" exclaimed Bella, looking with the most childish simplicity from the great thing in her hands to the boy's countenance.

"Yes, it was droll, wasn't it? And, my goodness, what a tool he'd got, Miss, hadn't he?"

"Immense," murmured Bella, thinking partly all the time of the thing she was skinning slowly backwards and forwards in her own hand.

"Oh, how you tickle me," sighed her companion, "what a beauty you are, how deliciously you rub it. Please, go on, Miss, I want to spend.''

"Do you, indeed," whispered Bella, "shall I make you spend?''

Bella saw the stiffened object reddening with the gentle titillation she was giving it, until the plump top looked almost ready to burst. The prurient idea to watch the effect of continued friction took violent possession of her.

She applied herself with redoubled energy to the lewd task.

"Oh, please, yes—go on; it is near coming. Oh! oh! How nice you do it; hold tight—go faster—skin it well down. Now, again. Oh! my goodness. Oh!

The long hard tool grew hotter and stiffer, as the little hands flew upon it.

"Ah! ugh!—It's coming!—Ugh! Hoo!" exclaimed the rustic lad, in broken accents, while his knees quivered, his body straightened his head rolled back, and amid contortions and stiffled cries his large and powerful penis squirted forth a rapid stream of thick fluid over the dear little hands which, eager to bathe themselves in the warm and slippery flood, now lovingly embraces the big shaft, and coaxed from it the fast out-pouring seminal shower.

Bella, suprised and delighted, pumped out every drop— she would have sucked it, had she dared—and then, drawing out her cambric handkerchief, she wiped the thick and pearly mess from her hands.

Then the youth, abashed and stupid, put up the expiring member, and regarded his companion with a mingled air of curiosity and wonder.

"Where do you live?" at last he found words to enquire.

"Not very far from here," replied Bella; "but you must not try to follow me, or to find out, you know; if you do," continued the young lady, "it will be the worse for you, for I shall never do that again, and you would be punished."

"Why don't we fuck like the stallion," suggested the youth whose ardour, only half appeased, began again to warm up.

"Some day, perhaps, not now, for I am in a hurry. I am late; I must go at once."

"Let me put my hand up your clothes? Say, when you will come again?"

"Not now," said Bella, withdrawing herself gradually, "but we will meet again."

She cherished a lively recollection of the stalwart affair in his breeches.

"Tell me," continued she, "have you ever—ever fucked."

"No, but I should like to. Don't you believe me? Well, then—yes, I have."

"How shocking," exclaimed the young lady.

"Father would like to fuck you," said he, without hesitation, taking no notice of her movement to depart.

"Your Father! Dreadful. How do you know that?"

"Because Father and I fuck the girls together. His tool is not bigger than mine."

"You say so, But do you really mean that your parent and you do such dreadful things in company?"

"Yes, when we get the chance. You should see him fuck. Oh! gum!" and he grinned idiotically.

"You don't seem a clever boy," said Bella.

"Father's not so clever as me," replied the lad, widening his grin, and showing his prick, again half stiff. "I know how to fuck now, though I only had it once. You should see me fuck."

And Bella saw the big stool pointing and throbbing.

"Whom did you do it with then? You naughty boy."

"A little girl of fourteen? Father and I both fucked her, and split her up."

"Which of you did it first?" demanded Bella.

"I did, and Father caught me. So then he wanted his

go, and made me hold her. You should see him fuck, my gum!''

A few minutes more Bella was again on her way, and seached her house without further adventures.

CHAPTER IX

When Bella related the result of her interview with Mr. Delmont that evening a low chuckle of delight escaped the lips of her two conspirators. She said nothing, however, of the young rustic she had encountered by the way. With that part of the day's performances she considered it quite unnecessary to trouble either the astute Father Ambrose, or her no less sagacious relative.

The plot was evidently about to thicken. The seed so discreetly sown would certainly fructify, and as Ambrose thought of the delicious treat which would certainly some day be his in the person of the beautiful young Julia Delmont, his spirits rose, and his animal passions fed by anticipation on the tender dainties hereafter to be his, until the result became visible in the huge distension of his member and the excitement which his whole manner betrayed.

Nor was Mr. Verbouc less touched. Sensual to the last degree, he promised himself a luscious repast on the newly opened charms of his neighbour's daughter, and the thought of the treat to come acted equally on his nervous temperament.

There were yet some details to arrange. It was clear that the simple Mr. Delmont would come to feel his way as to the truth of Bella's assertions respecting her Uncle's willingness to sell her maidenhead.

Father Ambrose, whose knowledge of the man had led him to suggest the idea to Bella, knew well with whom he was dealing—indeed, who did not exhibit his inmost nature to his holy man in the sacred right of confession that had the privilege to count him their confessor.

Father Ambrose was discreet, he faithfully observed the silence enjoined by his religion, but he made no scruple to use the facts he thus acquired for his own ends—and what those were the reader by this time knows as well as I did.

Thus the plot was arranged. Upon a certain day to be agreed upon, Bella was to invite her friend Julia to pass the day with her at her Uncle's house, and Mr. Delmont, it was intended, should be instructed to come and fetch her home. After a certain interval of flirtation between him and the innocent Bella, all being explained to him and previously arranged she was to withdraw, and under the pretext that it was absolutely necessary that some such precaution should be taken in order to avoid the possibility of scandal, she was to be presented to him in a convenient chamber recumbent upon a lounge, where her beautiful body and charms were to be at his disposal, while her head remained concealed behind a carefully closed curtain. Thus, Mr. Delmont, eager for the tender encounter, could snatch the jewel he coveted from the lovely victim, while she—ignorant of who her assailant might be—could never thereafter accuse him of the outrage or feel shame in his presence.

Mr. Delmont was to have all this explained to him, and his acquiescence was considered certain, only one reservation was intended: No one was to tell him that his own daughter was to be substituted in Bella's place. He would only know that when too late.

Meanwhile Julia was to be gradually prepared in secret for what was to take place, no mention, of course, being made of the final catastrophy, or the real participator in it. But here Father Ambrose felt himself at home, and by means of well directed enquiries, and at great deal of unnecessary explanation in the confessionnal, he soon brought the young girl to the knowledge of things of which she had never previously dreamed; all which Bella took care to explain and confirm.

All these matters had been finally disposed of in conference, and the consideration of the subject had produced by anticipation so violent an effect upon the two men, that they were now in train to enjoy their present good fortune in the possession of the fair young Bella with an amount of ardour they had never surpassed.

My young lady, on her side, was nothing loth to lend herself to their fantasies, and as she now sat or lay back on the soft lounge with a stiff standing member in either hand, her own emotions rose proportionately, until she longed for the vigorous embraces she knew were about to follow.

Father Ambrose, as usual, was the first. He turned her round, placed her on her belly, and directing her to extend her plump white buttocks as far back as possible, he stood for a moment contemplating the delicious prospect and the small and delicate slit which was just visible below. His weapon, redoutable as well provided with nature's essence, rose fiercely and menaced either entry into love's delightful shades.

Mr. Verbouc, as before, disposed himself to witness the disproportionate assault, with the evident intention of enjoying his favourite role afterwards.

Father Ambrose regarded, with a lecherous expression, the white and rounded promontories straight in front of him. The clerical tendencies of his education were exciting him to commit an infidelity to the Goddess, but the knowledge of what was expected of him by his friend and patron restrained him for the time.

"Delays are dangerous," said he, "my balls are very full, the dear child must have their contents, and you, my friend, must delight yourself with the abundant lubrication with which I shall provide you."

Ambrose, on this occasion at least, spoke nothing but the truth. His huge weapon, surmounted by the dull purple head, the broad proportions of which resembled the glowing ripeness of some fruit, stood stiffly up towards his navel, and his immense testicles, hard and round, appeared surcharged with the venomous liquor they were aching to discharge. A thick, opaque drop—an "avant-courrier" of that gush which was to follow—stood on the blunt apex of his penis, as, bursting with luxury, the satyr approached his prey.

Hastily bending down the stiff shaft, Ambrose put the big nut between the lips of Bella's tender slit and all anointed as it was, commenced to push it up her.

"Oh, how hard! How large you are!" cried Bella; "you hurt me; it is going in too far. Oh! stop!"

As well might have Bella appealed to the wind. A rapid succession of thrusts, a few pauses at intervals, more efforts, and Bella was impaled.

"Ah," exclaimed the ravisher, turning in triumph to his coadjutor, while his eyes sparkled and his lewd mouth watered with the pleasure he was having. "Ah, this is luscious, indeed; how tight she is, and yet she has it all. I am up her to my balls."

Mr. Verbouc took a careful survey. Ambrose was right. Nothing but his two huge balls remained visible of his genitals, and they were pressing close up between Bella's legs.

Meanwhile Bella felt the heat of the invader in her belly. She was sensible of the skinning and uncovering of the huge head within her, and instantly her lewdest emotions overtaking her, with a faint cry, she spent profusely.

Mr. Verbouc was delighted.

"Push! push!" said he, "she likes it now, give it her all—push!"

Ambrose needed no such incentive; seizing Bella round the hips, he buried himself in her at each bound. The pleasure rose upon him fast; he drew back, until he withdrew his smoking penis, all except the nut, and then lunging forward, he emitted a low groan, and squirted a perfect deluge of hot fluid into Bella's delicate body.

The girl felt the warm and trickling stuff shooting violently up her, and once more gave down her tribute. The great pushes which now came slopping into her vitals from the powerful stores of Father Ambrose, whose singular gift in this particular I have before explained, caused Bella the liveliest sensations, and she experienced the keenest pleasure during his discharge.

Scarcely had Ambrose withdrawn, than Mr. Verbouc took possession of his niece, and commenced a slow and delicious enjoyment of her most secret charms. After an interval of fully twenty minutes, during which time the salacious Uncle revelled in pleasure to his heart's content, he completed his gratification in a copious discharge, which Bella received with throbs of delight, such as no other than a thoroughly prurient mind could relish.

"I wonder," said Mr. Verbouc, after he had regained breath and refreshed himself with a large draught of rich wine. "I wonder how it is this dear child inspires me with such overwhelming rapture. In her arms I forget myself and all the world. The present intoxication of the moment carries me with it, and I enjoy I know not what of ecstasy."

The observation, or reflection, call it what you will, of the Uncle, was partly addressed to the good Father, and, no doubt, was partially the result of interior workings of the spirits which involuntarily rose to the surface and formed themselves into words.

"I could tell you. I think," said Ambrose sententiously, "only perhaps, you would not follow my reasoning."

"Explain, by all means," replied Mr. Verbouc. "I am all attention, and I should of all things like to hear your reason."

"My reason, or rather, I should say, my reasons," observed Father Ambrose, "are manifest when you are in possession of my hypothesis."

Then, taking a pinch of snuff, a habit which the good man usually indulged before delivering himself of any weighty reflections, he continued:

"Sensual pleasure must always be proportional to the adaptability of the circumstances which are intended to produce it. And this is paradoxical, because the more we advance in sensuality, and the more voluptuous our tastes grow, the greater becomes necessity that these circumstances should be themselves at variance. Do not misunderstand me; I will try to render myself more clear. Why does a man commit a rape when he is surrounded by woman willing to afford him the use of their bodies? Simply because he is not content to be in accord with the opposite party to his enjoyment, and it is her very unwillingness which constitutes his pleasure. No doubt there are instances in which a man of brutal mind, and seeking only his own sensual relief, where it is not possible to find a willing object to his gratification, forces a woman, or a child, to his will, with no other object than his immediate relief of those instincts which madden him, but search the record of such crimes, and you will find that by far the greater are the result of deliberate design, planned and executed in the face of obvious and even lawful means of gratification. The opposition to his proposed enjoyment serves to whet his lewd appetite, and the introduction of the featue of crime and violence add a zest to the matter which obtains a firm hold upon his mind. It is wrong, it is disallowed, therefore it is worth seeking, it becomes delicious. Again, what is the reason that a man of vigorous build, and capable of gratifying a fully developed woman, prefers a mere child of fourteen? I answer, because that very disparity affords him delight, gratifies the imagination, and constitutes that exact adaptability of circumstances of which I speak. In effect it is, of course, the imagination which is at work, The law of contrast is constant in this as in all else. The distinction merely of the sexes is not of itself sufficient to the educated voluptuary—there are needed further and special contrasts to perfect the idea he has conceived. The variations are infinite, but still the same law is traceable in all. Tall men prefer short women, fair men dark women, strong men select weak and tender women, and these women are fondest of vigorous and robust partners. Cupid's darts are tipped with incompatibilities and feathered with the wildest incongruities; none but the inferior animals, the brutes themselves, will copulate indiscriminately with the opposite sex, and even these have their preferences and desires as irregular as those of mankind. Who has not seen the unnatural conduct of a couple of street dogs, or laughed at the awkward efforts of some old cow, who driven to market with the common herd, vents her sensual instincts by mounting upon the back of her nearest neighbour? Thus I respond to your invitation, and thus I give you my reasons for your preference for your niece, for the sweet but forbidden playmate, whose delicious limbs I am now moulding."

As Father Ambrose concluded, he looked for an instant upon the fair girl, and his great weapon rose to its utmost dimensions.

"Come, my forbidden fruit," said he, "let me pluck you, let me revel in you to my heart's content. This is my pleasure—my ecstasy—my delirious enjoyment. I will swamp you in spunk, I will possess you in spite of the dictates of society—you are mine, come!"

Bella looked upon the ruddy and stiffened member of her confessor, she noted his excited gaze fixed upon her young body. She knew his intention, and prepared herself to gratify him.

Already had he frequently entered her tender belly and thrust the full length of that majestic penis into her small and sensible parts. Pain at the distention had now given way to pleasure, and young and elastic flesh opened to receive the column of gristle, with only just enough of uneasiness to make her careful in its reception.

The good man looked for a moment upon the tempting prospect before him, then advancing, he divided the rosy lips of Bella's slit, and pushed in the smooth gland of his great weapon: Bella received it with a shudder of mingled emotion.

Ambrose continued to penetrate until, after a few fierce thrusts, he buried his length in her tight young body, and she had him to the balls.

Then followed a series of pushes, of vigorous writhings on one part, and of spasmodic sobs and stiffled cries upon the other. If the pleasures of the holy man were intense, those of his youthful playmate were equally ecstatic, and his stiff affair was already well lubricated with her discharge, were, with a groan of intense feeling he once more reached his consummation, and Bella felt a flood of spendings burn violently into her vitals.

"Ah, how you have inundated me, both of you," said Bella, noticing as she spoke a large pool which covered her legs, and lay upon the sofa-cover between her things.

Before either could reply to the observation, a succession of cries made themselves heard in the quiet chamber, and becoming weaker and weaker as they continued, at once arrested the attention of all present.

And here I should acquaint my reader with one or two particulars which hitherto, in my crawling capacity. I have not thought it necessary to mention. The fact is that fleas, although no doubt agile members of society, cannot be everywhere at once, though no doubt they can, and do make up for this drawback by the exercise of an agility rarely equalled by others of the insect tribe.

I ought to have explained, like any human story writer, though, perhaps, with a circumlocution and more veracity, that Bella's aunt, Madame Verbouc, to whom my readers were very cursorily presented in the opening chapter of my history, occupied a chamber to herself in a wing of the mansion, where she spent much of her time, like Madame Delmont, in devotional exercises, and, with a happy disregard of mundane affairs, usually left all the domestic management of the house to her niece.

Mr. Verbouc had already reached the stage of indifference to the blandishments of his better half, and but seldom now visited her chamber or disturbed her repose for purposes of exercising his marital rights.

Madame Verbouc, however, was still young—only thirty-two summers had as yet passed over that pious and devout head—Madame Verbouc was handsome, and the lady had also brought her husband the additional advantage of a considerable fortune.

Madame Verbouc, in spite of her piety, sometimes languished for the more solid comforts of her husband's embraces. and relished with a keen delight the exercise of his rights and his occasional visits to her couch.

On this occasion Madame Verbouc had retired at her usual early hour, and the present digression is necessary to explain what follows. While this amiable lady, therefore, is engaged in those duties of the toilet which even fleas dare not profane, let us talk of another and no less important personage, whose conduct it will be necessary also to investigate.

Now it happened that Father Clement, whose exploits in the lists of the amorous Goddess we have already had occasion to chronicle, rankled under the fact of the young Bella's withdrawal from the Society of the Sacristy, and knowing well who she was, and where she was to be found, had for some days prowled about the residence of Mr. Verbouc to try and regain possession of so delicious a prize of which it will be remembered the cunning of Ambrose had deprived his "confreres".

In this attempt Clement was aided by the Superior, who also bitterly lamented his loss, without, however, suspecting the part that Father Ambrose had played.

On this particular evening Clement had posted himself near the house, and seeing an opportunity, set himself closely to watch a certain window which he made sure was that of the fair Bella.

How vain, indeed, are human calculations! While the forlorn Clement, robbed of his pleasures, was relentlessly watching one chamber, the object of his desires was bathed in salacious enjoyment between her two vigorous lovers in another.

Meanwhile the night advanced, and Clement finding all quiet, contrived to raise himself to the level of the window. A faint light was burning in the room, by which the anxious "cure" could detect a lady reposing by herself in the full enjoyment of sound slumber.

Nothing doubting of his ability to win Bella to his desires, could he only gain her ear, and mindful of the bliss he had already enjoyed while revelling in her beauties, the audacious scoundrel furtively opened the window and

entered the sleeping-chamber. Well wrapped in the flow-
ing frock of a monk, and disgulsed in its ample cowl, he
stole across to the bed; while his gigantic member, already
awake to the pleasures he promised himself, stood fiercely
up against his hirsute belly.

Madame Verbouc, roused from a pleasant dream, and
never doubting but that it was her faithful spouse who thus
so warmly pressed her, turned lovingly towards the intruder,
and, nothing loath, opened her willing thighs to his
vigorous attack.

Clement on his side, equally sure that the young Bella
was in his arms, and, moreover, not unwilling to admit his
caresses, pushed matters to a crisis, and mounting in hot
haste between the lady's legs, brought his huge penis
opposite the lips of a well-moistened slit, and fully aware
of the difficulties he expected to encounter in so young a
girl, thrust violently inwards.

There was a movement, another plunge downwards of
his big bottom, a gasp on the part of the lady, and slowly
but surely the gigantic mass hard flesh went in, until it was
fairly housed. Then, as it passed in for the first time
Madame Verbouc detected the extraordinary difference.
This penis was at least double the size of her husband's—to
doubt succeeded certainty. In the dim light she raised her
head; above was visible, close to her's, the excited visage
of the ferocious Clement.

Instantly there were a struggle, a violent outcry, and a
vain attempt to disengage herself from her strong assailant.

But come what might, Clement was in full possession
and enjoyment of her person. He never paused, but, on the
contrary, deaf to her cries, he broke in to his utmost
length, and strove, with feverish haste, to complete his

horrid triumph. Blind with rage and lust he was insensible to the fact of the opening of the door, of the blows which now rained upon his hinder parts, until with set teeth and the subdued roar of a bull, the crisis seized him, and he poured a torrent of semen into the unwilling womb of his victim.

Then he awoke to the position, and fearing the results of his detestable outrage, he rose in all haste, and withdrawing his foaming weapon, slipped from the bed upon the side opposite his asailant. Dodging as well as he could the cuts which Mr. Verbouc aimed at him and keeping the hood of his frock over his features to avoid detection, he rushed toward the window by which he had entered, then taking a headlong leap he made good his escape in the darkness, followed by the imprecations of the infuriated husband.

We have already stated in a former chapter that Mrs. Verbouc was an invalid, that is, she fancied herself one, and to a person of weak nerves and retiring habits my reader may picture for himself what was likely to be her condition after undergoing so indelicate an outrage. The enormous proportions of the man, his strength, his fury almost killed her, and she lay without consciousness on the couch which had witnessed her violation.

Mr. Verbouc was not naturally endowed with astonishing attributes of personal courage and when he beheld the assailant of his wife rise satisfied from the pursuit, allowed Clement to retreat in peace.

Meanwhile Father Ambrose and Bella, following at a respectful distance from the outraged husband, witnessed from the half-opened door the denouement of the strange scene.

As soon as the ravisher rose, Bella and Ambrose both instantly recognised him; indeed, the former had had, as the reader knows already, good reason to remember the huge lolling member which dangled dripping between his legs.

Mutually interested in maintaining silence, a look exchanged between them was sufficient to indicate the necessity for reserve, and they withdrew before any movement on the part of the outraged woman betrayed their proximity.

It was several days before poor Mrs. Verbouc was well enough to leave her bed. The shock to her nerves had been dreadful, and nothing but the kind and conciliatory manner of her husband enabled her to hold her up at all.

Mr. Verbouc had his own reasons for letting the matter pass, and he allowed no considerations beyond expediency to weigh with him.

On the day after the catastrophe I have recorded above, Mr. Verbouc received a visit from his dear friend and neighbour Mr. Delmont, and after being closeted with him for over an hour, the two parted with beaming smiles and the most extravagant compliments.

The one had sold his niece, and the other believed he had purchased that precious jewel: A maidenhead.

When Bella's uncle made the announcement that evening that the bargain had been struck, and the affair duly arranged, there was great rejoicing among the conspirators.

Father Ambrose immediately took possession of the maidenhead, and driving in to the girl the whole length of his member, proceeded, as he explained it, to keep the place warm, while Mr. Verbouc, reserving himself, as usual, until his "confrere" had done, afterwards attacked the same mossy fort, as he facetiously expressed it, just to oil the passage for his friend.

Then the whole of the details were finally arranged, and the party broke up, confident in the success of their stratagem.

CHAPTER X

Ever since the meeting in the green lane with the rustic whose simplicity had so much interested her. Bella had dwelt upon the expressions he had used, and the extraordinary avowal of his parent's complicity in his sensuality. It was clear that his mind was simple almost to idiocy, and from his remark; "Father's not so clever as me," she assumed that the complaint was congenital, and wondered if the father really possessed the same, or—as declared by the boy—even greater proportions in his organs of generation.

I plainly saw, by her habit of thinking partly aloud, that Bella did not reckon upon her Uncle's opinion, or stand any longer in fear of Father Ambrose. She was doubtless resolved to follow her own course, whatever it might be, and I was not, therefore, at all astonished when I found her wending her way the following day at about the same hour in the direction of the meadows.

In a field hard by the spot where she had beheld the sexual encounter between the horse and his mate, Bella discovered the lad engaged in some simple agricultural operation, and with him was another person, a tall and remarkably dark man, of about forty-five years of age.

Almost as soon as she saw them, the lad observed the young lady, and running toward her, after apparently a word of explanation with his companion, he showed his delight by a broad grin.

"That's Father," said he, pointing over his shoulder, "come and frig him."

"For shame, you naughty boy," said Bella, much more inclined to laugh than to be angry. "How dare you use such language?"

"What did you come for?" asked the boy. "Did you come for fucking?"

By this time they had reached the man, who stuck his spade into the ground, and began to grin at the girl in very much the same fashion as his son.

He was strong and well built, and by his manner Bella could see the boy had told him the particulars of their first meeting.

"Look at Father, ain't he a randy one?" remarked the youth. "Ah! You should see him fuck!"

There was no attempt at disguise; the two evidently understood each other and grinned more than ever. He seemed to accept it as a huge compliment, but he cast his eyes upon the delicate young lady, the like of whom he had probably never met before, and it was impossible to mistake the look of sensuous longing which shone in his large black eyes.

Bella began to wish she had never come.

"I should like to show you Father's big doodle," said the lad. and suiting the action to word, he commenced to unbutton the trousers of his respectable parent.

Bella covered her eyes, and made a movement in retreat. Instantly the son stepped behind her. Her refuge in the lane was thus cut off.

"I should like to fuck you," exclaimed the Father, in a hoarse voice. "Tim would like to fuck you as well, so you must not go away yet. Stop and be fucked!"

Bella was really frightened.

"I cannot," she said; "indeed you must let me go. You must not hold me like that: you must not drag me along; let me go. Where are you taking me?"

There was a small building in the corner of the field, and they were now at the door. Another second and the pair had pushed her inside and shut the door, lowering a large wooden bar across it afterwards as they entered.

Bella looked round and saw that the place was clean and half-filled with hay in trusses. She saw that resistance would be useless. It would be best to be quiet, and perhaps, after all, the strange pair would not hurt her. She noticed however, that the trousers of both stuck out in front, and doubted but that their ideas were in harmony with their excitement.

"I want you to see Father's cock; my gum! you ought to see his cods, too."

Once more the lad began unbuttoning his father's breeches. Down went the flap and out stuck his shirt with something under it, which caused it to bunch up in a curious manner.

"Oh, do hold still, Father," whispered the son; "let the lady see your doodle."

With that he raised the shirt, and exposed in Bella's face a fiercely erected member with a broad plum-like nut, very red and thick, but not of very unusual length. It had a considerable bend upwards, and the head, which divided down the middle by the tightness of the frenum, bent still further back towards his hairy belly. The shaft was immensely thick, rather flat and hugely swollen.

The girl felt her blood tingle as she looked upon it. The nut was a large as an egg—plump, and quite purple. It emitted a strong smell. The lad made her approach, and pressed her white, lady-like little hand upon it.

"Didn't I tell you it was bigger than mine," continued the boy, "look here; mine is not nearly as thick as Father's."

Bella turned. The boy had his trousers open and his formidable penis in full view. He was right—it could not compare with his father's for size.

The older of the two now caught her round the waist. Tim also essayed to cling to her, and to get his hand under her clothes. Between them she swayed to and fro. A sudden push cast her upon the hay. Then up went her skirts. Bella's dress was light and wide, she wore no drawers. No sooner did the two catch sight of her plump, white legs than they snorted again, and both threw themselves on her together. A struggle now ensued. The Father, much heavier and stronger than the boy, got the advantage.

His breches were about his heels; his big, fat prick was out and wagged within three inches of her navel. Bella opened her legs, she longed for a taste of it. She put down her hand. It was hot as fire, and as hard as a bar of iron. Mistaking her intention, the man rudely withdrew her arm, and roughly helping himself, put the tip of his penis to the pink lips. Bella opened her young parts all in her power, and with several forcible lunges the peasant got about halfway in. Here his excitement overcame him, and a terher. He discharged violently, getting right up rible stream of very thick fluid spouted into her as he did so until the big nut lay against her womb, and he sent a quantity of his semen into it.

"Eh, you are killing me," cried the girl, half smothered, "what is all that you are pouring into me?"

"That's the spunk; that's what that is," remarked Tim, as he bent down and watched the operation delightedly. "Didn't I tell you, he was a good' un to fuck."

Bella thought the man would now get off, and allow her to rise, but she was mistaken; the large member which was now crammed into her only seemed to grow more rigidly stiff, and to stretch her worse than ever.

Presently the peasant began to work himself up and down, pushing cruelly into Bella's young parts at each descent. His enjoyment appeared to be extreme. The discharge which had already taken place caused his truncheon to slip in and out without difficulty, and made the soft region foam with the rapid movement.

Bella gradually became dreadfully excited. Her mouth opened, her legs went up and her hands were convulsively clenched on either side. She now favoured every effort and delighted to feel the fierce plunges with which the sensual fellow buried his reeking weapon in her young belly.

For a quarter of an hour the conflict raged on both sides. Bella had discharged frequently, and was on the point of giving down a warm emission, when a furious spouting of semen rushed from the man's member and inundated the young lady's parts.

The fellow then rose, and withdrawing his dripping prick, from which the last drops of his plentiful ejection were still exuding, he stood moodily contemplating the panting figure he had released.

Still threatening stood his huge rammer in front of him, yet smoking from the warm sheath, Tim, with true filial care, proceeded to wipe it tenderly and return it, pendant and swollen with its late excitement, within his father's shirt and breeches.

This done, the lad began to cast sheep's eyes on Bella, who still remained, slowly recovering herself upon the hay. Looking and feeling, Tim who met with no resistance, commenced to push his fingers about in the region of the young lady's private parts.

The father now came forward, and taking his son's weapon in his grasp, began to frig it up and down. It was already stiffly erected, and presented a formidable mass of flesh and muscle in Bella's face.

"Goodness me. I hope you are not going to put that into me," murmured Bella.

"I am, though," answered the lad, with one of his silly grins. "Father frigs me, and I like it, and now I mean to fuck you."

The father guided this splitter towards the girl's thighs. Her slit, already swimming in the spendings which the peasant had thrown into it, quickly received the ruby nut. Tim gushed it in, and stooping over her, shoved in the long shaft, until his hairs rubbed Bella's white skin.

"Oh, it's dreadfully long," cried she; "you are shockingly big, you naughty boy. Don't be so violent. Oh, you kill me! How you push. Oh! you can't get in any further; pray be gentle; there, it's quite up me. I can feel it up to my waist. Oh, Tim, you horrid, bad boy!"

"Give it to her," muttered the father, who was feeling the lad's balls, and tickling all round between his legs all the time. "She'll take it. Tim. Ain't she a beauty? What a tight little cunt she's got, ain't she, boy?"

"Ugh, don't talk, Father, I can't fuck."

For some minutes there was silence, save for the noise of the two heaving, struggling bodies in the hay. After a while the boy stopped. His prick, though hard as iron and stiff as wax, had not apparently spent a drop. Presently, Tim pulled it right out, all smacking and glistening with moistures.

"I can't spend," said he, mournfully.

"It's the frigging," explained the Father. "I frig him so often that he misses it now."

Bella lay panting and all exposed.

The man now applied his hand to Tim's cock, and began vigorously rubbing it up and down.

The girl expected every moment he would spend in her face.

After a while passed in thus further exciting his son, the father suddenly applied the burning nut to Bella's slit, and as it passed up, a perfect deluge of sperm issued from it and flooded her interior. Tim set himself to work to writhe and struggle, and ended by biting her in the arm.

When this discharge had quite terminated, and the last throb had passed through the boy's huge rammer, he slowly drew it out and let the girl rise.

They had no intention, however, to let her go, for after

undoing the door, the boy looked cautiously round, and then replacing the wooden bar, turned to Bella.

"What fun, wasn't it," he remarked. "I told you Father was good at it, didn't I?"

"Yes, you did, indeed, but you must let me go now; do, there's a good boy."

A grin was the only response.

Bella looked towards the man, and what was her terror to see him in a state of nudity, all save his shirt and boots, and with an erection that threatened another and even fiercer assault upon her charms.

His member was literally livid with the tension and stuck up against his hairy belly. The head had swollen enormously with the previous irritation, and from its tip a glistening drop hung pendant.

"You'll let me fuck you again," enquired the man, as he caught the young lady by the waist and put her hand on his tool.

"I'll try," murmured Bella, and seeing there was no help for it, she suggested his sitting on the hay, while straddling across his knees, she tried to insert the mass of gristly flesh.

After a few heaves and pushes it went in, and a second course, no less violent than the first commenced. A full quarter of an hour elapsed. It was now apparently the elder who could not be brought to the point of emission.

"How tiresome they are," thought Bella.

"Frig it, my dear," said the man, withdrawing from her body his member, even harder than before.

Bella clasped it with both her small hands and worked it up and down. After a little of this excitement she stopped, and perceiving a small spurt of semen exude from the urethra, she quickly placed herself upon the huge pummel, and had hardly housed it before a flood of spunk rushed into her.

Bella rose and fell, thus pumping him, till all was finished, after which they let her go.

At length the day arrived, the eventful morning broke, when the beautiful Julia Delmont was to lose that coveted treasure which is so eagerly sought after on the one hand, and often so thoughtlessly thrown away upon the other.

It was still early, when Bella heard her foot upon the stairs, and the two friends were no sooner united than a thousand pleasant subjects of prattle found their way into their talk, until Julia began to see that there was something which Bella was keeping back. In fact, her rapidity was simply a mask for the concealment of some piece of news which she was somewhat reluctant to break to her companion.

"I know you have something to tell me, Bella, there is something I have not heard yet which you have to tell me; what is it, darling."

"Can't you guess," she said, with a wicked smile playing round the dimpling corners of her rosy lips.

"Is it anything about Father Ambrose?" asked Julia. "Oh! I feel so dreadfully and awkward, when I see him now, and yet he told me there was no harm in what he did."

"Nor more there was, depend upon it; but what did he do?"

"Oh, more than ever. He told me such things, and then he put his arm round my waist, and kissed me, till he almost took my breath away."

"And then," suggested Bella.

"How can I tell you, dearest! Oh, he said and did a thousand things, until I thought I was going out of my senses."

"Tell me some of them at least."

"Well, you know that, after he had kissed me so hard, he put his fingers down my dress, and then he played with my foot and my stocking, and then he slipped his hand up higher, until I thought I was going to faint."

"Oh! you little wanton, I feel sure you liked his proceedings all the while."

"Of course I did. How could I do otherwise? He made me feel as I had never felt in my life before."

"Come, Julia, that was not all—he did not stop there, you know."

"Oh no; of course he did not, but I cannot tell you his next proceeding."

"Away with such childishness," cried Bella, pretending to be piqued at her friend's reticence. "Why not avow all to me?"

"If I must, I suppose there is no help for it, but it seemed so shocking, being all so new to me, and yet not wrong. After he had made me feel as if I was dying of a delicious shivering sensation, which his fingers produced, he suddenly took my hand in his and placed it upon something he had which felt like a child's arm. He bid clasp me it tightly. I did as he directed me, and then looking down, I beheld a great red thing, all white skin and blue veins, with a funny, round purple top, like a plum. Well, I saw that this thing grew out from between his legs, and that it was covered below with a great mass of curly black hair."

Julia hesitated. "Go on," said Bella.

"Well, he kept my hand upon it, making me rub it over and over; it was so large, and stiff, and hot!"

"No doubt it was under the excitement of such a little beauty."

"Then he took my other hand a\d placed both together on his hairy thing. I felt so frighter ed when I saw how his eyes glared and his breathing grew hard and quick. He reassured me. He called me his dear child, and, rising, bade me fondle the stiff thing in my bosom. It stuck out close to my face."

"Is that all?" asked Bella, persuasively.

"No, no, indeed it is not, but I feel so ashamed. Shall I go on? Is it right that I should divulge these things? Well then, after I had held this monster in my bosom a little time, during which it throbbed and pressed me with a warm delightful pressure, he asked me to kiss it. I complied at once. A warm sensuous smell arose from it, as I pressed my lips upon it. At his request I continued kissing it. He bade me open my lips and rub the top between them. A moisture came at once upon my tongue, and on an instant a thick gush of warm fluid ran into my mouth, and spurted over my face and hands. I was still playing with it, when a noise of a door opening at the other end of the church obliged the good Father to put away what I had hold of—"for," he said, "it is not for the common people to know what you know, or to do what I permit you to do. His manner was so kind and obliging, and he made me think I was quite different to all the other girls. But tell me, Bella, dearest, what is the mysterious news you have to tell me? I am dying to know."

"Answer me first, whether or not the good Ambrose told you of joys—of pleasures, derived from the object you trifled with, and whether he pointed out any means by which such delights could be indulged without sin?"

"Of course he did—he said that in certain cases such indulgence became a merit."

"As in marriage, for instance, I suppose."

"He said nothing about that, except that marriage often brought much misery, and that even marriage vows might, under certain circumstances, be broken advantageously."

Bella smiled. She recollected to have heard somewhat the same strain of reasoning from the same sensual lips.

"Under what circumstances did he mean then that these joys were permitted?"

"Only when the mind was firmly set upon a good motive, beyond the actual indulgence itself, and that, he says, can only he, when some young girl, selected from others for the qualities of her mind, is dedicated to the relief of the servants of religion."

"I see," said Bella, "go on."

"Then he said how good I was, and how meritorious it would be for me to exercise the privilege he endowed me with, and devote myself to the sensuous relief of himself and others, whose vows prevented them from either marrying or otherwise gratifying the feeling which natnre has implanted in all men alike. But tell me, Bella, you have some news for me—I know you have."

"Well, then, if I must—I must, I suppose. Know then, that good Father Ambrose has arranged that it will be best for you to be initiated at once, and he has provided for it here to-day."

"Oh, me! You don't say so! I shall be so ashamed, so dreadfully shy."

"Oh, no, my dear, all that has been thought of. Only so good and considerate a man as our dear Confessor could have so perfectly arranged everything as he has done. It is designed that the dear man shall be able to enjoy all beauties your witching little self can afford him, while, to make a long matter short, he will neither see your face, nor you his."

"You don't say so! In the dark, then, I suppose?"

"By no means; that would be to forego all the pleasures of sight, and he would lose the rich treat of looking upon those delicious charms the dear man has set his heart upon possessing."

"How you make me blush, Bella—but how, then, is it to be?"

"It will be quite light," explained Bella, with the air of a mother to her child. "It will be in a nice little chamber we have; you will be laid upon a convenient couch, and your head will be passed through and concealed by a curtain, which so fills a door-way leading into an inner apartment that only your body, all naked to the view, will be exposed to your ardent assailant."

"Oh, for shame! Naked, too!"

"Oh, Julia my dear, tender Julia," murmured Bella, as a shudder of keen ecstatic feeling rushed through her, "what delights will be yours; how you will awake to the delicious joys of immortals, and find now that you are approaching that period called puberty, the solaces of which I know you already stand in need of."

"Oh, don't Bella, pray, don't say that."

"And when at length," continued her companion, whose imagination had already led her into a reverie to which outward impressions were quite imperious, "when at length the struggle is over, the spasms arrive, and that great throbbing thing shoots out its viscid stream of maddening delight, oh! then she will join that rush of ecstasy, and give down her virgin exchange."

"What are you murmuring about?"

Bella roused herself.

"I was tinking," she said, dreamily, "of all the joys of which you were about to partake."

"Oh, don't," Julia exclaimed, "you make me blush, when you say such dreadful things."

Then followed a further conversation, in which many small matters had their place, and while it was in progress I found an opportunity to overhear another dialogue, quite as interesting to me, but of which I shall only furnish the summary for my readers.

It took place in the library, and occured between Mr. Delmont and Mr. Verbouc. They had evidently understood each other on the main points at issue, which incredible as they may appear, were the surrender of Bella's person to Mr. Delmont in consideration for a certain round sum to be then and there paid down, and afterwards invested for the benefit of "his dear niece," by the indulgent Mr. Verbouc.

Knave and sensualist as the man was, he could not quite bring himself to the perpetration of so nefarious a transaction without some small sop to stay the conscience of even so unscrupulous a being as himself.

"Yes," said the good and yielding uncle, "the interests of my niece are paramount, my dear sir. A marriage is not unlikely hereafter, but the small indulgence you demand is, I think, well compensated for between us, as men of the world, you understand, purely as men of the world, by a sum sufficient to reward her for the loss of so fragile a possession."

Here he laughed, principally because his matter-of-fact and dull-witted guest failed to understand him.

Thus it was settled, and there remained only the preliminaries to arrange. Mr, Delmont was charmed, ravished out of his somewhat heavy and stolid indifference, when he was informed that the bargain was forthwith to be executed, and that he was to take possession of that delicious virginity he had so longed to destroy.

Meanwhile the good, dear, generous Father Ambrose had been some time in the house and had prepared the chamber where the sacrifice was to take place.

Here after a somptuous breakfast, Mr. Delmont found himself with only a door between him and the victim of his lust.

Who that victim was, he had not the remotest idea. He only thought of Bella.

The next moment he had turned the lock and entered the chamber, the gentle warmth of which refreshed and stimulated the sensual instincts about to be called into play.

Ye Gods! What a sight burst upon his enraptured vision. Straight before him, reclining upon a couch, and utterly nude, was the body of a young girl. A glance sufficed to demonstrate the fact that it was beautiful, but it would have taken several minutes to go over in detail and discover all the separate merits of each delicious limb and member: The well-rounded limbs, childlike in their plump proportions; the delicate bosom just ripening into two of the choicest and whitest little hills of soft flesh; the roseate buds which tipped their summits; the blue veins which coursed and meandered here and there and showed through the pearly surface like little rivulets of sanguine fluid only to enhance the more the dazzling whiteness of the skin. And then, oh! then, the central spot of man's desire, the rosy close-shut lips where nature loves to revel, whence she springs and whither she returns—Ia source—it was there visible in its almost infantine perfection.

All indeed was there except—the head. That all-important member was conspicuous by its absence, and yet the gentle undulations of the fair maiden plainly evidenced that she suffered no inconvenience by its non-appearance.

Mr. Delmont exhibited no astonishment at this phenomenon. He had been prepared for it, and also enjoined to maintain the strictest silence. He therefore busied himself to observe and delight himself with such charms as were prepared for his enjoyment.

Meanwhile no sooner had he recovered from his surprise and emotion at the first view of so much naked beauty, than he found certain evidences of its effects upon those sensuous organs which so readily respond in men of his temperament to emotions calculated to produce them.

His member, hard and swollen, now stood out in his breeches and threatened to burst from its confinement. He, therefore, liberated it, and allowed a strong but gigantic weapon to spring into light, and rear its red head in presence of its prey.

Reader, I am only a flea. I have but limited powers of perception, and I fail in ability to describe the gentle gradations and soft creeping touches by which this enraptured ravisher approached his conquest. Revelling in his security, Mr. Delmont ran his eyes and his hands over all. His fingers opened the delicate slit, over which as yet only a soft down had made its appearance, while the girl, feeling the intruder in her precints, wriggled and twisted to avoid, with the coyness natural under the circumstances, his wanton touches.

But now he draws her to him; his hot lips press the soft belly—the tender and sensitive nipples of her young breasts. With eager hand he firmly seizes her swelling hip, and pulling her towards him, opens her white legs and plants himself between.

Reader, I have already remarked I am only a flea. Yet

fleas have feelings, and what mine were I will not attempt to describe when I beheld that excited member brought close to the pouting lips of Julia's moist slit. I closed my eyes; the sexual instincts of the male flea rose within me, and I longed—yes! how ardently I longed to be in Mr. Delmont's place.

Meanwhile steadily and sternly he proceeded in his work of demolition. With a sudden bound he essayed to penetrate the virgin parts of the young Julia. He fails—he tries again, and once more his baffled engine flew up and lay panting on the heaving belly of his victim.

During this trying period no doubt Julia must have spoilt the plot by an outery more or less violent, but for a precaution adopted by that sage demoraliser and priest, Father Ambrose.

Julia had been drugged.

Once more Mr. Delmont returned to the charge. He pushes, he forces forward, he stamps his feet upon the floor, he rages and he foams, and oh, God! the soft elastic barrier gives way and he goes in—in with a felling of ecstatic triumph; in, until the pleasure of the tight and moist compression forces from his sealed lips a groan of pleasure. In, until his weapon, buried to the hair which covered his belly, lay throbbing and swelling yet harder and longer in its glove-like sheath.

Then followed a struggle no flea can describe—sighs of blissful and ravishing sensations escape his open slobbering lips, he pushes, he bends forward, his eyes turn up, his mouth opens, and, unable to prevent the rapid completion of his lustful pleasures, the strong man gasps out his soul, and with it a torrent of seminal fluid, which thrown well forward squirts into the womb of his own child.

All this time Ambrose had been a hidden spectator of

the lustful drama, and Bella had operated on the other side of the curtain to prevent any approach to utterance on the part of her young visitor.

This precaution was, however, unnecessary; for Julia, sufficiently recovered from the effects of the narcotic to feel the smart, had fainted.

CHAPTER XI

No sooner was the struggle over, and the victorious, rising from the quivering body of the girl, began to recover himself from the ecstasy into which so delicious an encounter had thrown him, than suddenly the curtain was slid on one side, and Bella herself appeared in the opening.

If a cannon-shot had suddenly passed close to the astonished Mr. Delmont, it could not have occasioned him one half the consternation which he felt, as hardly believing his own eyes, he stood, open-mouthed, alternately regarding the prostate body of his victim, and the apparition of her he supposed he had so recently enjoyed.

Bella, whose charming "neglige" set off to perfection her young beauties, affected to appear equally stupified, but apparently recovering herself, she drew back a step, with a well-acted expression of alarm.

"What—what is all this?" inquired Mr. Delmont, whose agitation had prevented him from remembering that he had not as yet even readjusted his clothes, and that a very important instrument in the gratification of his late sensual impulse hung, still swollen and slippery, fully exposed between his legs.

"Heavens! that I should have made such a dreadful mistake," cried Bella, hiding her furtive glances this inviting exhibition.

"Tell me, for pity's sake, what mistake, and who then, is this?" exclaimed the trembling ravisher pointing, as he spoke, to the recumbent nudity before him.

"Oh, come—come away," cried Bella, hastily moving towards the door, and followed by Mr. Delmont, all anxiety for an explanation of the mystery.

Bella led the way into an adjoining boudoir, and closing the door firmly, she threw herself upon a luxuriously disposed couch, so as to exhibit freely her beauties, while she pretended to be too overwhelmed with her horror to notice the indelicacy of her pose.

"Oh! what have I done! what have I done!" she sobbed, hiding her face in her hands in apparent anguish.

A horrible suspicion flashed across the mind of her companion; he gasped out, half choking with emotion.—

"Speak—who is that—who?"

"It was not my fault—I could not know that it was you they had brought here for me, and—and—not knowing better—I substituted Julia.

Mr. Delmont staggered back—a confused sense of something dreadful broke upon him—a distress obstructed his vision, and then gradually he awake to the full sense of the reality. Before, however, he could utter a word, Bella, well instructed as to the direction his ideas would take, hastened to prevent him time to think.

"Hush! she knows nothing of it—it has been a mistake—a dreadful mistake, and nothing more. If you are disappointed, it has been my fault—not yours; you know I never thought for a moment it was to have been you. I think," she added, with a pretty pout, and a significant side-glance at the still protruding member, "it was very unkind of them not to have told me it was to have been you."

Mr. Delmont saw the beautiful girl before him; he could not but admit to himself that, whatever pleasures might have been his in the involuntary incest in which he had been a party, they had, nevertheless, failed of his original intention, and lost something for which he had paid so dearly.

"Oh, if they should find out what I have done," murmured Bella, changing a little her position, and exposing a portion of one leg above the knee.

Mr. Delmont's eyes glittered in spite of himself his calmness returned, his animal passions were asserting themselves.

"If they should find me out," again sighed Bella, and with that she half rose and threw her beautiful arms round the neck of the deluded parent.

Mr. Delmont pressed her in a close embrace.

"Oh, my goodness, what is this?" whispered Bella,

whose little hand had seized the slimy weapon of her companion, and was now engaged in squeezing and moulding it in her warm grasp.

The wretched man felt all her touches, all her charms, and, once more rampant with lust, sought no better fate than to revel in her young virginity.

"If I must yield," said Bella, "be gentle with me; oh! how you touch me! Oh! take away your hand. Oh! heavens! What do you do?"

Bella had only time to catch a glimpse of his red-headed member, stiffer and more swollen than ever, and the next moment he was upon her.

Bella made no resistance, and fired by her loveliness, Mr. Delmont quickly found the exact spot, and taking advantage of her inviting position, pushed with fury his already lubricated penis into her young and tender parts.

Bella groaned.

Further and further inwards went his hot dart, until their bellies met together, and he was up her body to his balls.

Then commenced a rapid and delicious encounter, in which Bella did her part to perfection, and roused by this new instrument of pleasure, went off in a torrent of delight. Mr. Delmont quickly followed her example, and shot into Bella a copious flood of his prolific sperm.

For several moments both lay without motion, bathed in the exudation of their mutual raptures, and panting with their efforts, until a slight noise made itself heard, and before either had attempted to withdraw, or change from the very unequivocal position they occupied, the door of the boudoir opened, and three persons made their appearance almost simultaneously.

These were Father Ambrose, Mr. Verbouc, and the gentle Julia Delmont.

The two men appeared bearing between them the half-conscious figure of the young girl, whose head, languidly falling on one side, lay on the shoulders of the robust priest, while Verbouc, no less favoured by his proximity, supported her slender form with her nervous arm, and gazed in her face with a look of unsatisfied lust, such as only a devil incarnate could have equalled. Both men were in a state of hardly decent dishabille, and the unfortunate little Julia was as naked as when, scarcely a quarter of an hour before, she had been violently ravished by her own father.

"Hush!" whispered Bella, putting her hand upon the lips of her amorous companion, "for God's sake, do not criminate yourself. They cannot know who has done it; better suffer all than confess such a dreadful fact. They are merciless—beware, how you thwart them."

Mr. Delmont instantly saw the truth of Bella's prediction.

"See, thou man of lust," exclaimed the pious Ambrose, "behold the state in which we found this dear child," and placing his big hand upon the beautiful unflegded "motte" of the young Julia, he wantonly exhibited his fingers, reeking with the paternal discharge to the others.

"Horrible," observed Verbouc, "and if she should be found with child!"

"Abominable," cried Father Ambrose. "We must, of course, prevent that."

Delmont groaned.

Meanwhile Ambrose and his coadjutor led their beautiful young victim into the apartment, and commenced to cover her with those preliminary touches and lascivious pawings which precede the unbridled indulgence in luxurious possession. Julia, half awake from the effects of the sedative they had given her, and wholly confounded by the proceedings of the virtuous pair, appeared barely conscious of the presence of her parent, while that worthy, held in position by the white arms of Bella, still lay soaking on her soft white belly.

"The spunk running down her legs," exclaimed Verbouc, eagerly inserting his hand between Julia's thighs; "how shocking!"

"It is even reached her pretty little feet," observed Ambrose, raising one of her rounded legs, under pretence of making an examination of the delicate kid-boot, upon which he had truly observed more than one gout of seminal fluid, while, with a glance of fire, he eagerly explored the rosy chink thus exposed to view.

Delmont groaned again.

"Oh, good Lord, what a beauty!" cried Verbouc, smacking the rounded buttocks. "Ambrose, proceed to prevent any consequences from so unusual a circumstance. Nothing less than a second emission from another and vigorous man can render such a thing positively safe."

"Yes, she must have it—that is certain." muttered Ambrose, whose state during all this time may be better imagined than described.

His cassock stuck out in front—his whole manner betrayed his violent emotions. Ambrose lifted his frock, and gave liberty to his enormous member, the ruby and inflamed head of which seemed to menace the skies.

Julia, horribly frightened, made a feeble movement to escape. Verbouc, delighted, held her in full view.

Julia beheld for the second time, the fiercely erected member of her Confessor, and knowing his intention from the previous initiation she had passed through, half fainted with trembling fear.

Ambrose, as if to outrage the feelings of both, father

and daughter, exposed fully his huge genitals and wagged his gigantic penis in their faces.

Delmont, overcome with terror, and finding himself in the hands of the two cospirators, held his breath and cowered by the side of Bella, who, delighted beyond measure by the success of the scheme, kept counselling him to remain neutral and let them have their will.

Verbouc, who had been fingering the moistened parts of the little Julia, now yielded her to the furious lust of his friend, and prepared himself for his favourite pastime of watching her violation.

The Priest, beside himself with lubricity, divested himself of his nether garments, and his member, standing grimly all the while, proceeded to the delicious task which awaited him. "She is mine at last," he murmured.

Ambrose immediately seized his prey; he passed his arms around her, and lifted her from the ground; he bore the trembling Julia to an adjoining sofa, and threw himself upon her naked body; he endeavoured with all his might to accomplish his enjoyment. His monstrous weapon, hard as iron, battered at the little pink slit, which although already lubricated with the semen she had received from Mr. Delmont, was no easy sheath for the gigantic penis which threatened her.

Ambrose continued his efforts. Mr. Delmont could only see a heaving mass of black silk, as the robust figure of the priest writhed upon the form of his little daughter. Too experienced to be long held in check, however. Ambrose felt himself gaining ground, and too much master of himself to allow the pleasure to overtake him too soon, he now bore down all opposition, and a loud shriek from Julia announced the penetration of the huge rammer.

Cry after cry succeeded, until Ambrose, at length firmly

buried in the belly of the young girl, felt he could go no further, and commenced those delicious pumping movements, which were to end at the same moment his pleasure and the torture of his victim.

Meanwhile Verbouc, whose lustful emotions had been intensily excited by the scene between Mr. Delmont and Julia, and subsequently by that between the foolish man and his niece, now rushed towards Bella, and releasing her from the relaxing embrace of his unfortunate friend, at once opened her legs, regarded for a moment her reeking orifice, and then at one bound buried himself in an agony of pleasure in her belly, well anointed by the abundance of spunk which had been already discharged there. The two couples now performed their delicious copulation in silence, save for the groans which came from the half-murdered Julia, the stentorous breathing of the fierce Ambrose, or the grunts and sobs of Mr. Verbouc. Faster and more delicious grew the race, Ambrose, having forced his gigantic penis up to the curling mass of black hair which covered its root into the tight slit of the young girl, became perfectly livid with lust. He pushed, he drove, he tore open with the force of a bull; and had not nature at length asserted herself in his favour by bringing his ecstasy to a climax, he must have succumbed to his excitement in an attack which would probably have for ever prevented a repetition of such a scene.

A loud cry came from Ambrose. Verbouc well knew its import, he was discharging. His rapture served to quicken his own. A howl of passionate lust arose within the chamber as the two monsters loaded their victims with their seminal outpourings. Not once, but three times did the Priest shoot his prolific essence into the very womb of the tender girl, before he assuaged his raging fever of desire.

As it was, to say that Ambrose simply discharged would give but a faint idea of the fact. He positively spurted his semen into the little Julia in thick and powerful jets, uttering all the while groans of ecstasy, as each hot and slippery injection rushed along his uge urethra and flew in torrents into the stretched receptacle. It was some minutes ere all was over, and the brutal Priest arose from his torn and bleeding victim.

At the same time Mr. Verbouc left exposed the opened thighs and besmeared slit of his niece, who lying still in the dreamy trance which follows the fierce delight, took no heed of the thick exuding drops which formed a white pool upon the floor between her well-stockinged legs.

"Ah, how delicious," exclaimed Verbouc, "you see, there is pleasure after all in the path of duty, Delmont, is there not?" turning to that dumbfounded individual. "If Father Ambrose and myself had not mixed our humble offerings with that prolific essence of which you seem to have made such good use, there is no knowing what mischief might have ensued. Oh, yes, nothing like doing the thing which is right, eh, Delmont?"

"I don't know. I fell ill; I am in a kind of dream, yet I am not insensible of sensations which cause me renewed delight. I cannot doubt your friendship—your secrecy. I have much enjoyed, I am still excited, I know not what I want?—Say, my friends."

Father Ambrose approached, and laying his big hand on the shoulder of the poor man, he encouraged him with a few whispered words of comfort.

As a Flea I am not at liberty to mention what these were, but their effect was to dissipate in a great measure the cloud of horror which oppressed Mr. Delmont. He sat down and gradually grew more calm.

Julia also had now recovered, and seated on each side of the burly priest, the two young girls ere long felt comparatively at ease. The Holy Father spoke to them like a father and he drew Mr. Delmont from his reserve, and that worthy having copiously refreshed himself with a considerable libation of rich wine, began to evince evident pleasure in the society in which he found himself.

Soon the invigorating effects of the wine began to tell upon Mr. Delmont. He cast wistful and envious glances towards his daughter. His excitement was evident, and showed itself in the bulging of his garments.

Ambrose perceived his desire and encouraged it. He led him to Julia, who, still naked, had no means of concealing her charms. The parent looked on all with an eye in which lust predominated. A second time would not be so very much more sinful, he thought.

Ambrose nodded his encouragement. Bella unbuttoned his nether garment, and taking his stiff prick in her hand, squeezed it softly.

Mr. Delmont understood the position, and the next moment was upon his child. Bella guided the incestuous member to the soft red lips; a few pushes and the half-maddened father was fully entered in the belly of his pretty child.

The struggle that followed was intensified by the circumstances of his horible connection. After a fierce and rapid course, Mr. Delmont discharged and his daughter received in the utmost recesses of her young womb the guilty spendings of her unnatural parent.

Father Ambrose, whose sensual character thoroughly predominated, owned one other weakness, and that was ~hing; he would preach by the hour together, not so much on religions subjects as on others much more mundane, and certainly not usually sanctioned by Holy Mother Church.

On this occasion he delivered discourse which I found it impossible to follow, and went to sleep in Bella's armpit until he had done.

How far in the future this consummation would have been, I know not, but the gentle Bella, having obtained a hold of his great lolling affair in her little white hand, so pressed and tickled it that the good man was feign to pause by reason of the sensation she produced.

Mr. Verbouc also, who, it will be remembered coveted nothing so much as a buttered bun, knew only too well how splendidly buttered were the delicious little parts of the newly-convered Julia. The presence of the father also— worse than helpless to prevent the utmost enjoyment of his child by these two libidinous men, served to whet his appetite while Bella, who felt the slime oozing from her warm slit, who also conscious of certain, longings which her previous encounters had not appeased.

Verbouc commenced again to visit with his lascivious touches the sweet and childish charms of Julia, impudently moulding her round buttocks and slipping his fingers between their rounded hillocks.

Father Ambrose, not less active, had got his arm round Bella's waist, and putting her half-nude form close to him, he sucked licentious kisses from her pretty lips.

As the two men continued these toyings, their desires proportionately advanced until their weapons, red and inflamed by previous enjoyments, stood firmly in the air, and stiffly menaced the young creatures in their power.

Ambrose, whose lust never wanted much incentive, quickly possessed himself of Bella, who, nothing loth, let him press her down upon the sofa which had witnessed already two encounters, and still further exciting his skinned and flaming pego, the daring girl let it enter between her white thigs, and favouring the disproportionate attack as much as she could, she received its whole terrible build in her moistened slit.

This sight so worked upon the feelings of Mr. Delmont, that he evidently needed small encouragement to attempt a second "coup" when the Priest had done.

Mr. Verbouc, who had for some time been throwing lascivious glances towards Mr. Delmont's young daughter, now found himself once more in condition to enjoy. He reflected that the repeated violation she had already experienced at the hands of her father and the Priest had fitted her for the part he loved to play, and he knew, both by touch and sight, that her parts were sufficiently oiled by the violent discharges she had received to gratify his dearest whim.

Verbouc gave a glance towards the Priest, who was now engaged in the delicious enjoyment of his niece, and then closing upon the beautiful Julia, he in his turn, succeeded in reversing her upon a couch and with considerable effort thrust his stout member to the balls in her delicate body.

This new and intensified enjoyment brought Verbouc to the verge of madness; he pressed himself into the tight and glovelike slit of the young girl, and throbbed all over with delight.

"Oh, she is heaven itself!" he murmured, pressing in his big member to the balls, which were gathered up tightly below. "Good Lord, what tightness—what slippery pleasure—ugh!" and another determined thrust made poor Julia groan again.

Meanwhile Father Ambrose, with eyes half shut, lips parted, and nostrils dilated, was battering the beautiful parts of the young Bella, whose sensual gratification became evident in her sobs of pleasure.

"Oh! my goodness! You are—you are too big—enormous! Your great thing. Oh! it's up to my waist. Oh, oh! it's too much; not so hard—dear Father—how you push!—you will kill me. Ah! gently—go slower—I feel your great balls at my bottom."

"Stop a moment," cried Ambrose, whose pleasure had become insupportable, and whose spunk was nearly provoked to rush out of him. "Let us pause, Shall I change with you, my friend? The idea is lovely."

"No, oh, no! I cannot move, I can only go on—this dear child is perfect enjoyment."

"Be still, Bella, dear child, or you will make me spend. Don't squeeze my weapon so rapturously."

"I cannot help it—you kill me with pleasure. Oh! go on, but gently. Oh, not so hard! Don't push so fiercely. Heavens! he's going to spend. His eyes close, his lips open. My God! you kill me—you slit me up with that big thing. Ah1 oh! come then! spend, dear—Father—Ambrose. Give me the burning spunk. Oh! push now—harder—harder— kill me, if you like."

Bella threw her white arms round his brawny neck, opened wide her soft and beautiful thighs, and took in his huge instrument, until his hairy belly rubbed on her downy mount.

Ambrose felt himself about to go off in rapturous emission right into the body of the girl under him.

Push—push now!" cried Bella, regardless of all modesty, and giving down her own discharge in spasms of pleasure. "Push—push—drive it up me. Oh, yes, like that. Ah, God, what a size! What a length—you slit me, brute that you are. Oh, oh! oh! You are off—I feel it. Oh, God—what spunk! Oh, what gushes!''

Ambrose discharged furiously, like the stallion that he was, thrusting with all his might into the warm belly below.

He then reluctantly withdrew, and Bella, released from his clutches, turned to regard the other pair. Her uncle was administering a shower of short thrusts at her little friend, and it was evident a climax must soon be put to his enjoyment.

Meanwhile Julia, whose recent violation and subsequent hard treatment by the brutal Ambrose had sadly hurt and enfeebled, had not the slightest pleasure, but lay a unresisting and inert mass in the arms of her ravisher.

When therefore, after a few more pushes, Verbouc fell forward in a voluptuous discharge, she was only aware that something warm and wet was being rapidly injected into her, without experiencing any other sensations than languor and fatigue.

Another pause followed this third outrage, during which Mr. Delmont subsided into a corner and appeared to be dozing. A thousand pleasantries now took place. Ambrose, while reclining upon the couch, made Bella stride over him, and applying his lips to her reeking slit, luxuriated in kisses and touches the most lascivious and depraved.

Mr. Verbouc, not to be behindhand with his companion, played off several equally libidinous inventions upon the innocent Julia.

The two then laid flat upon a couch, and felt all her beauties over, lingering with admiration upon her yet un-fledged ''motte,'' and the red lips of her young cunt.

After a time the desires of both were seconded by the

outward and visible signs of two standing members, eager again for a taste of pleasures so ecstatic and select.

A new programme was now, however, to be inaugurated. Ambrose was the first to propose it. "We have had enough of their cunts," said he, coarsely, turning to Verbouc, who had passed over to Bella, and was playing with her nipples. "Let us try what their bottoms are made of. This lovely little creature would be a treat for the Pope himself, and ought to have buttocks of velvet and a "derriere" fit for an Emperor to spend into."

The idea was instantly seized upon, and the victims secured. It was abominable, it was monstrous, it was apparently impossible, when viewed in all its disproportionate character. The enormous member of the Priest was presented to the small aperture of Julia's posterior—that of Verbouc threatened his niece in the same direction. A quarter of an hour was consumed in the preliminaries and after a frightful scene of lust and lechery, the two girls received in their bowels the burning jets of these impious discharges.

At length a calm succeeded to the violent emotions which had overwhelmed the actors in this monstrous scene.

Attention was at length directed to Mr. Delmont.

That worthy, as I have before remarked, was quietly ensconsed in a corner, apparently overcome with sleep, or wine, or possibly both.

"How quiet he is," observed Verbouc.

"An evil conscience is a sad companion," remarked Father Ambrose, whose attentions were directed to the ablution of his lolling instrument.

"Come, my friend—it is your turn now, here is a treat for you," continued Verbouc, exhibiting to the edification of all the most secret parts of the almost insensible Julia;

"come and enjoy this.—Why, what is the matter with the man? Good heavens, why,—how—what is this?"

Verbouc recoiled a step.

Father Ambrose leant over the form of the wretched Delmont—he felt his heart. "He is dead," he said, quietly—and so it was.

CHAPTER XII

Sudden death is so common an event, especially among persons whose previous history has led to the supposition of the existence of some organic deterioration, that surprise easily gives place to ordinary expressions of condolence, and this again to a state of resignation at a result by no means to be wondered at.

The transition may be thus expressed:

"Who would have thought it?"

"Is it possible?"

"I always had my suspicions."

"Poor fellow!"

"Nobody ought to be surprised!"

This interesting formula was duly gone through when poor Mr. Delmont paid the debt of nature, as the phrase goes.

A fortnight after that unfortunate gentleman had departed this life, his friends were all convinced they had long ago detected symptoms which must sooner or later prove fatal; they rather prided themselves on their sagacity, reverently admitting the inscrutability of Providence.

As for me, I went about much as usual, except that for a change I fancied Julia's legs had a more piquant flavour than Bella's and I accordingly bled them regularly for my repast matutinal and nocturnal.

What could be more natural than that Julia should pass much of her time with her dear friend Bella, and what more likely than that the sensual Father Ambrose and his patron, the lecherous relative of my dear Bella, should seek to improve the occasion and repeat their experiences upon the young and docile girl!

That they did so, I knew full well, for my nights were most uneasy and uncomfortable, always liable to interruption from the incurasions of long hairy tools among the pleasant groves, wherein I had temporarily located myself, and frequently nearly drowning me in a thick and frightfully glutinous torrent of animal semen.

In short, the young and impressionable Julia was easily and completely broken up, and Ambrose and his friend revelled to their heart's content in her complete possession.

They had gained their ends, what mattered the sacrifice to them?

Meanwhile other and very different ideas were occupying the mind of Bella, whom I had abandoned, and feeling, at length, a degree of nausea from the too frequent indulgence in my new diet, I resolved to vacate the stockings of the pretty Julia and return—''Revenir a mon mouton,'' as I might say—to the sweet and succulent pastures of the prurient Bella.

I did so, and ''voici le resultat!''

One evening Bella retired to rest rather later than usual. Father Ambrose was absent upon a mission to a distant parish, and her dear and indulgent uncle was laid up with a sharp attack of gout, to which he had lately become more subject.

The girl had already amanaged her hair for the night. She had also denuded herself of her upper garments and was in the act of putting her ''chemise de nuit'' over her head, in the process of which she inadvertently allowed her petticoats to fall and display before her glass the beautiful proportions and exquisitely soft and transparent skin.

So much beauty might have fired Anchorite, but alas! there was no such ascetic there present to be inflamed. As for me, she only nearly broke my longest feeler and twisted my right jumper, as she whirled the warm garment in the hair above her head.

One present there was, however, whom Bella had not counted upon, but upon whom, it is needless to say, nothing was lost.

And now I must explain that ever since the crafty Father Clement had been denied Bella's charms, he had sworn a very unclerical and beastly oath to renew the attempt to surprise and capture the pretty fortress he had once already stormed and ravished. The remembrance of his happiness brought tears into his sensual little eyes, and a certain distension sympathetically imparted itself to his enormous member.

Clement in fact had sworn a fearful oath to fuck Bella in a natural state in her own unvarnished words, and I, Flea though I be, heard and understood their import.

The night was dark; the rain fell—Ambrose was absent. Verbouc was ill and helpless—Bella would be alone—all this was perfectly well-known to Clement, and accordingly he made the attempt. Improved by his recent experience in his geography of the neighbourhood, he went straight to the window of Bella's chamber, and finding it, as he expected, unfastened and open, he coolly entered and crept beneath the bed. From this position Clement beheld with throbbing veins the toilette of the beautiful Bella until the moment when she commenced to throw off her chemise, as I have already explained. In so doing Clement saw the nudity of the girl in full view, and snorted internally like a bull. From his recumbent position he had no difficulty in viewing the whole of her body from the waist down, and as she faced from him, his eyes glistened as he saw the lovely twin globes of her bottom opening and shutting as the graceful girl twisted her lithe figure in the act of passing the chemise over her head.

Clement could restrain himself no longer; his desires rose to boiling point, and softly, but swiftly, gliding from his concealment, he arose behind her; and without an instant's loss of time he clasped her asked body in his arms, placing as he did so, one of his fat hands over her rosy mouth.

Bella's first instinct was to scream, but that feminine resource was denied her. Her next was to faint, and this she probably would have done out for one circumstance. This was the fact, that as the audacious intruder held her close to him, a certain something, hard, long and warm, very sensibly pressed inwards between her smooth buttocks, and lay throbbing in their separation and up along her back. At this critical moment Bella's eyes encountered their image reflected in the opposite toilet-glass, and she recognized, over her shoulder the inflamed and ugly visage, crowned by the shock circle of red hair, of the sensual priest.

Bella understood the situation in the twinkling of an eye. It was nearly a week since she had received the embraces of either Ambrose or her uncle, and this fact had no doubt something to do with the conclusion she formed on this trying occasion. What she had been on the point of doing in reality, the lewd girl now only simulated.

She allowed herself to recline gently back upon the stout figure of Clement, and that happy individual, believing she was really fainting, at once withdrew his hand from her mouth and supported her in his arms.

The unresisting position of so much loveliness excited Clement almost to madness. She was nearly naked, and he ran his hands over her polished skin. His immense weapon, already stiff and distended with impatience, now palpitated with passion, as he held the beautiful girl in his close embrace.

Clement tremblingly drew her face to his, and imprinted a long and voluptous kiss upon her sweet lips.

Bella shuddered and opened her eyes.

Clement renewed his caresses.

The young girl sighed.

"Oh!" she exclaimed, softly, "how dare you come here? Pray, pray leave me at once—it is shameful."

171

Clement grinned. He was always ugly—now he looked positively hideous in his strong lust.

"So it is, said he, "shameful to treat such a pretty girl like this, but then, it's so delicious, my darling."

Bella sobbed.

More kisses, and a roving of hands over the naked girl. A great uncouth hand settled over the downy mount, and a daring finger, separating the dewy lips, entered the warm slit and touched the sensitive clitoris.

Bella closed her eyes, and repeated the sigh. That sensitive little organ instantly commenced to develop itself. It was by no means diminutive in the case of my young friend, and under the lascivious fingering of the ugly Clement, it arose, stiffened, and stuck out, until it almost parted the lips of its own accord.

Bella was fired—desire beamed in her eyes; she had caught the infection and stealing a glance at her seducer, she noticed the terrible look of rampant lust which spread itself over his face, as he toyed with her secret young charms.

The girl trembled with agitation; an earnest longing for the pleasure of coition took absolute possession of her, and unable longer to control her desires, she quickly insinuated her right hand behind her, and grasped, but could not span, the huge weapon which drove against her bottom.

Their eyes met—lust raged in each. Bella smiled, Clement repeated his sensual kiss, and insinuated his lolling tongue within her mouth. The girl was not slow to second his lecherous embraces, and allowed him full liberty of action, both as to his roving hands and active kisses. Gradually he pressed her towards a chair, and Bella, sinking upon it, awaited impatiently the next overtures of the Priest.

Clement stood exactly in front of her. His cassock of black silk, which reached to his heels, bulged out in front, while his cheeks, fiery red with the violence of his desires, were only rivalled by the smoking lips, as he breathed excitedly in the ecstasy of the anticipations.

He saw that he had nothing to fear and everything to enjoy.

"This is too much," murmured Bella, "go away."

"Oh! impossible now I have had the trouble of getting here."

"But you may be discovered, and I should be ruined."

"Not likely—you know we are quite alone and not at all likely to be disturbed. Besides, you are so delicious, my child, so fresh, so young and beautiful—there, don't withdraw your leg. I was only putting my hand on your soft thigh. In fact, I want to fuck you, my darling."

Bella saw the huge projection give a flip up.

"How nasty you are!—What words you use."

"Do I, my little pet, my angel," said Clement, again seizing on the sensitive clitoris, which he moulded between his finger and thumb; "they are all prompted by the pleasure of feeling this pouting little cunt that is slyly trying to evade my touches."

"For shame!" exclaimed Bella, laughing in spite of herself.

Clement came close and stopped over her, as she sat; he took her pretty face between his fat hands. As he did so, Bella was conscious that his cassock, already bulging out with the force of the desires communicated to his truncheon, was within a few inches of her bosom.

She could detect the throbs with which the black silk garment gradually rose and fell. The inclination was irresistible; she put her delicate little hand under the priest's vestment, and lifting up sufficiently felt a great hairy mass, which contained two balls, as large as fowl's eggs.

"Oh, my goodness, how enormous!" whispered the young girl.

"All full of the beautiful thick spunk," sighed Clement, playing with the two pretty breasts which were so close to him.

Bella shifted her ground, and once more grasped with both hands the strong and stiffened body of an enormous penis.

"How dreadful, what a monster!" exclaimed the lewd girl. "It is a big one, indeed; what a size you are!"

"Yes, isn't that a cock?" observed Clement, pushing forward and holding up his cassock the better to bring the gigantic affair into view.

Bella could not resist the temptation, but raising still higher the man's garment, released his penis entirely, and exposed it at full stretch.

Fleas are bad measures of size and space, and I forbear to give any exact dimensions of the weapon upon which the young lady now cast her eyes. It was gigantic, however, in its proportions. It had a large and dull red head, which stood shining and naked at the end of a long grissly shaft. The hole at the tip, usually to small, was, in this instance, a considerable slit, and was moist with the seminal humidity which gathered there. Along the whole shaft coursed the swollen blue veins, and behind all was a matted profusion of red bristling hair. Two huge testicles hung below.

"Good heavens! Oh, Holy Mother!" murmured Bella, shutting her eyes, and giving it a slight squeeze.

The broad, red head, distended and purple with the effect of the exquisite tickling of the girl, was now totally uncapped, and stood stiffly up from the folds of loose skin, which Bella pressed back up(n the great white shaft. Bella toyed delightfully with this acquisition, and pressed still further back the velvety skin beneath her hand.

Clement sighed.

"Oh, you, delicious child," "he said gazing at her with sparkling eyes; "I must fuck you at once, or I shall throw it all over you."

"No, no you must not waste any of it," exclaimed Bella; "how pressed you must be to want to come so soon."

"I cannot help it—pray, remain quiet a moment, or I shall spend."

"What a big thing—how much can you do?"

Clement stopped and whispered something into the girl's ear, which I could not catch.

"Oh, how delicious, but it is incredible."

"No, it is true, only give me the chance. Come, I am longing to prove it to you, pretty one—see this! I must fuck you!"

He shook the monstrous penis, as he stood in front of her. Then, bending it down, he suddenly let it go. It sprung up, and as it did so, the skin went back of its own accord, and the big red nut came out with the hand-open urethra exuding a drop of semen.

It was close below Bella's face. She was sensible of a faint, sensuous odour, which came up from it and increased the disorder of her sense. She continued to finger and play with it.

"Stop, I entreat you, my darling, or you will waste it in the air."

Bella remained quiet a few seconds. Her warm band still clasped as much as she could of Clement's prick. He amused himself meanwhile in moulding her young breasts, and in working his fingers up and down in her moist cunt. The play made her wild. Her clitoris grew hot and prominent; her breathing became hard and her pretty face flushed with longing.

Harder and harder grew the nut, it shone like a ripe plum. Bella's was crimson with desire; she furtively regarded the ugly man's naked and hairy belly—his brawny thighs, thickly covered also with hair like an ape. His great cock, each moment more swollen, menaced the skies, and caused her indescribable emotions.

Excited beyond measure, she wound her white arms around the stout figure of the great brute and covered him with rapturous kisses. His very ugliness increased her libidinous sensations.

"No, you must not waste it, I cannot let you waste it," and then, pausing for a second, she moaned with a peculiar articulation of pleasure, and lowering her fair head, opend her rosy mouth, and instantly received as much of the lascivious morsel as she could cram into it.

"Oh! how nice; how you tickle—what—what pleasure you give me."

"I will not let you waste it. I will swallow every drop," whispered Bella, raising her mouth for a moment from the glistening nut.

Then again sinking her face forward, she pressed her pouting lips upon the big tip, and parting them gently and delicately, received the orifice of the wide urethra between them.

"Oh, Holy Mother!" exclaimed Clement, "this is heaven! How I shall spend? Good Lord? how you tickle and suck."

Bella applied her pointed tongue to the orifice and licked it all round.

"How nice it tastes; you have already let out a drop or two."

"I cannot continue, I know I cannot," murmured the Priest, pushing forward and tickling with his finger at the same time the swollen clitoris that Bella put within his reach. Then she retook the head of the great cock again between her lips, but she could not make the whole of the nut enter her mouth, it was so monstrously large.

Tickling and sucking—passing back in slow delicious movements the skin which surrounded the red and sensitive ridge of his tremendous thing, Bella now evidently invited the result she knew could not long be delayed.

"Ah, Holy Mother! I am almost coming; I feel—I—Oh! oh! now suck. You've got it."

Clement lifted his arm in the air, his head fell back, his legs straddled wide apart, his hands worked convulsively, his eyes turned up, and Bella felt a strong spasm pass through the monstrous cock. The next moment she was almost knocked backwards by a forcible gush of semen, which rushed spouting in a continuous stream from his genitals, and flew in torrents down her gullet.

In spite of all her wishes and endeavours, the greedy girl could not avoid a stream issuing from the corners of her mouth while Clement, beside himself with pleasure, kept pushing forward in sharp jerks, each one of which sent a fresh jet of spunk down her throat. Bella followed all his movements, and held fast hold of the streaming weapon until all was done.

"How much did you say?" muttered she, one "tea-cup full—there were two."

"You beautiful darling," exclaimed Clement, when at last he found breath. "What divine pleasure you have given me. Now it is my turn, and you must let me examine all I love in those little parts of yours."

"Ah, how nice it was; I am nearly choked." cried Bella. "How slippery it was, and, oh, goodness, what a lot!"

"Yes. I promised you plenty, my pretty one, and you so excited me that I know you must have received a good dose of it. It ran in streams."

"Yes, indeed it did."

"Now I am going to suck your pretty cunt, and fuck you deliciously afterwards."

Suiting the action to the word, the sensual Priest threw himself between Bella's milk white thighs, and thrusting his face forward, plunged his tongue between the lips of the pinky slit. Then rolling it around the stiffened clitoris, he commenced a titillation so exquisite that the girl could hardly restrain her cries.

"Oh, my goodness. Oh, you suck my life out. Oh! I am—I am going off. I spend!" and, with a sudden forward movement towards his active tongue, Bella emitted most copiously upon his face, and Clement received all he could catch in his mouth with the delight of an epicure.

At length the Priest arose; his big weapon which had scarcely softened, had now resumed its virile tension, and stuck out from him in a terrible erection. He positively snorted with lust, as he regarded the beautiful and willing girl.

"Now I must fuck you," said he, as he thrust her towards the bed. "Now I must have you, and give you a taste of this cock in your little belly. Oh, what a mess there'll be!"

Hastly throwing off his cassock and nether garments, he compelled the sweet girl like-wise to denude herself of her chemise, and then the great brute, his big body all covered with hair and brown as a mulatto, took the lily form of the beautiful Bella in his muscular arms and tossed her lightly on the bed. Clement regarded for a moment her extended figure as, palpitating with mingled desire and terror, she awaited the terrible onslaught; then he looked complacently upon his tremendous penis, erect with lust, and hastily mounting, threw himself upon her, and drew the bed-clothes over him.

Bella, half-smothered beneath the great hairy brute, felt his stiff cock interposed between their bellies. Passing down her hand, she touched it again.

"Good heavens! what a size, it will never go into me."

"Yes, yes—we will get in, all of it, up to the balls, only you must help, or I shall probably hurt you."

Bella was saved the trouble of a reply, for the next moment an eager tongue was in her mouth and almost choking her.

Then she became aware that the Priest had raised himself slightly, and that the hot head of his gigantic cock was pressing inwards between the moist lips of her little rosy slit.

I cannot go through the gradations of that preliminary conjuncture. It was full ten minutes in the accomplishment, but in the end ungainly Clement lay buried to the balls in the pretty body of the girl, while with her soft legs raised and thrown over his brawny back she received his lascivious caresses, as he gloated over his victim and commenced those lustful movements with the intention of ridding himself of his scalding fluid.

At least ten inches of stiff nervous muscle lay soaking and throbbing in the little girl's belly, while a mass of coarse hair pressed the battered and delicate mount of poor Bella.

"Oh, my! Oh! my, how you hurt," moaned she. "My Good! you are splitting me up."

Clement moved.

"I can't beat it—you are too big, indeed. Oh! take it out. Ah, what thrusts."

Clement pushed mercilessly two or three times.

"Wait a second, my little devil, until I smother you with my spunk. Oh, how tight you are. How you seem to suck my cock,—There, it's in now, You have it all."

"Oh, mercy."

Clement thrust hard and rapidly—push followed push—he squirmed and writhed on the soft figure of the girl. His lust rose hot and furious. His huge penis was strained to bursting in the intensity of his pleasure, and tickling, maddening delight of the moment.

"Ah, now I am fucking you at last."

"Fuck me," murmured Bella, opening still wider her pretty legs, as the intensity of the sensations gained upon her. "Oh, fuck me hard—harder," and with a deep moan of rapture she deluged her brutal ravisher with a copious discharge, pushing upwards at the same moment to meet a dreadful lunge. Bella's legs were jerked up and down, while Clement thrust himself between, and forced his long, hot member in and out in luscious movements. Soft sighs, mingled with kissings from the set lips of the lusty intruder, occasioned moans of rapture, and the rapid vibrations of the bedstead all bespoke the excitement of the scene.

Clement needed no invitation. The emission of his fair companion had supplied him with the moistening medium he desired, and he took advantage of it to commence a radid series of in and out movements, which caused Bella as much pleasure as pain.

The girl seconded him with all her power. Gorged to repletion, she heaved and quivered beneath his sturdy strokes. Her breath came in sobs, her eyes closed in the fierce pleasure of an almost constant spasm of emission. The buttocks of her ugly lover opened and shut, as he strained himself at every lunge into the body of the pretty child.

After a long course he paused a moment.

"I can't hold any longer, I'm going to spend. Take my spunk, Bella, you will have floods of it, pretty one."

Bella knew it—every vein in his monstrous cock was swollen to its utmost tension. It was insupportably big. It ressembled nothing so much as the gigantic member of an ass.

Clement began to move again—the saliva ran from his mouth; with an ecstatic sensation. Bella awaited the coming seminal shower.

Clement gave one or two short, deep thrusts, then groaned and lay still, only quivering slightly all over.

Then a tremendous spout of semen issued from his prick and deluged the womb of the young girl. The big brute buried his head in the pillows and forced himself in with his feet against the bedsteadend.

"Oh, the spunk," screamed Bella "I feel it. What streams, Oh, give it me. Holy Mother! What pleasure it is!"

"There, there, take that," cried the Priest, as once more at the first rush of semen into her, he pushed wildly up her belly, sending at each thrust a warm squirt of semen into her.

"There, there. Oh, what pleasure!"

Whatever had been Bella's anticipations, she had had no idea of the immense quantity this stalwart man could discharge. He pumped it out in thick masses, and splashed it into her very womb.

"Oh, I am spending again," and Bella sank half-fainting beneath the strong man, while his burning fluid continued still to dart from him in viscid jets.

Five times more that night Bella received the glutinous contents of Clement's big balls, and had not daylight warned them it was time to part, he would have recommenced.

When the astute Clement cleared the house, and hastened, as the day broke, to his humble quarter, he was forced to admit he had had his belly full of pleasure, even as Bella had had her belly full of spunk. As for that young lady, it was lucky for her that two protectors were incapacited, or they must have discovered in the painful and swollen condition of her young parts, that an interloper had been trespassing on their preserves.

Youth is elastic—everyone says so. Bella was young and "very elastic." If you had seen Clement's immense machine you would have said so. Her natural elasticity enabled her not only to sustain the introduction of this battering-ram, but also in about a couple of days to fell none the worse for it.

Three days after this interesting episode Father Ambrose returned. One of his first cares was to seek Bella. He found her, and invited her to follow to a boudoir.

"See," cried he producing his tool, inflamed and standing at attention, "I have had no amusement for a week, my cock is bursting, Bella, dear."

Two minutes later her head was reclining on the table of the apartment, while, with her clothes thrown completely over her head, and her swelling posteriors fully exposed, the salacious Priest regarded her round buttocks, and slapped them vigorously with his long member. Another minute and he had pushed his instrument into her from behind, until his black frizzly hair pressed against her bottom. Only a few thrusts brought from him a gush of spunk, and he sent a shower up to her waist.

The good Father was too much excited by long abstinence to lose his rigidity, but drawing down his stalwart tool, he presented it, all slippery and smoking, at the tight little entrance between those delicious buttocks. Bella favoured him, and well-amointed as he was, he slipped in, and gave her another tremendous dose from his prolific testicles. Bella felt fervent the discharge, and welcomed the hot spunk, as he discharged it up her bowels. Then he turned her over on the table, and sucked her clitoris for a quarter of an hour, making her discharge twice in his mouth, at the end of which time he employed her in the natural way.

Then Bella went to her chamber and purified herself, and, after a slight rest, put on her walking dress and went out.

That evening Mr. Verbouc was reported worse, the attack had reached regions which caused serious anxiety to his medical attendant. Bella wished her uncle a good night and retired.

Julia had installed herself in Bella's room for the night, and the two young friends, by this time well-enlightened as to the nature and properties of the male sex, lay exchanging ideas and experiences.

"I thought I was killed," said Julia, "when Father Ambrose pushed that great ugly thing of his up my poor little belly, and when he finished I thought he was in a fit, and could not understand what that slippery warm stuff could be which kept splashing into me, but, oh!''

"Then my dear, you commenced to feel the friction on that sensitive little thing of yours, and Father Ambrose's hot spunk spurted all over it."

"Yes, that it did. I am always smothered, Bella, when he does it."

"Hush! What was that?"

Both the girls sat up and listened. Bella, better accustomed to the peculiarities of her chamber than Julia could be, turned her attention to the window. As she did so, the shutter gradually opened, and there appeared a man's head.

Julia saw the apparition, and was just about to scream, when Bella motioned her to keep silence.

"Hush! Dont't be alarmed," whispered Bella, "he won't eat us, only it's too bad to disturb one in this cruel fashion."

"What does he want?" asked Julia, half hiding her pretty head under the clothes, but keeping a bright eye all the time upon her intruder.

All this time the man was preparing to enter, and having sufficiently opened the shutter he squeezed his large figure through the opening, and alighting on the middle of the floor, disclosed the bulky form and ugly sensual features of Father Clement.

"Holy Mother! a Priest," exclaimed Bella's young visitor, "and a fat one, too. Oh! Bella, what does he want?"

"We shall soon see what he wants," whispered the other.

Meanwhile Clement had approached the bed.

"What? Is it possible? a double treat," he exclaimed; "delightful Bella, this is indeed, an unexpected pleasure."

"For shame, Father Clement,"

Julia had disappeared under the bed-clothes.

In two minutes the Priest had stripped himself of his raiment, and without so much as waiting for an invitation, darted in the bed.

"Oh, my!" cried Julia, "he's touching me."

"Ah, yes, we shall both be touched, that is certain," murmured Bella, as she felt Clement's huge weapon pressing close up to her back. "What a shame for you to come in here without any permission."

"Shall I go then, pretty one?" said the Priest, putting his stiff tool into Bella's hand.

"You may stay, now you're here."

"Thank you," whispered Clement lifting one of Bella's legs, and inserting the big head of his cock from behind.

Bella felt the thrust and mechanically seized Julia round the loins.

Clement thrust once more, but Bella, with a sudden bound, jerked him out. Then she rose, turned back the clothes, and exposed both the hairy body of the Priest, and also the fairy form of her companion.

Julia turned instinctively, and there, right under her nose, was the stiff and standing penis of the good Father, looking ready to burst with the luxurious proximity in which its owner found himself.

"Touch it," whispered Bella.

Nothing daunted, Julia grisped it in her little white hand.

"How it throbs! It is getting bigger and bigger, I declare."

"Swing it down," murmured Clement; so—oh! lovely!"

Both girls now sprang out of bed, and eager for the fun, commenced stroking and skinning the Priest's huge penis, until he was almost with his eyes turned up, and a slight convulsive spending.

"This is heaven!" said Father Clement movement of his fingers, which betokened his pleasure.

"Stop now, darling, or else he'll spend," remarked Bella, assuming an air of experience, to which no doubt, her previous acquaintance with the monster she considered fairly entitled her.

But Father Clement himself was in no humour to waste his shot, while two such pretty targets were ready for his aim. During the fingering to which the girls subjected his cock, he had remained impassive, but now, gently drawing the young Julia towards him, he deliberately raised her chemise and exposed all her secret beauties to view. He allowed his eager hands to pat and mould her lovely butocks and thighs and opened with his thumbs her rosy chink; he thrust his lewd tongue within, and sucked exciting kisses from her very womb.

Julia could not remain insensible under such treatment, and when at last, trembling with desire, and rampant with lust, the daring Priest threw her back upon the bed, she opened her young thighs and let him see the crimson lining of her tight-fitting slit. Clement got between her legs, and throwing them up, he touched with the big top of his member the moistened lips. Bella now assisted, and taking the immense penis in her pretty hand, skinned it back and presented the tip fairly at the orifice.

Julia held her breath and bit her lip. Clement gave a hard thrust. Julia, brave as a lioness, held firm. In went the head, more thrusts, more pressures, and in less time than it takes to write it, Julia was gorged with the Priest's big member.

Once fairly in possession of her body, Clement commenced a regular series of deep thrusts, and Julia, with indescribable sensations, threw back her head and covered her face with one hand, while with the other she clasped Bella's wrist.

"Oh! it is enormous; but what pleasure he is giving me!"

"She's got it all; he is in up to his balls," exclaimed Bella.

"Ah! how delicious! She'll make me spend—I can't help it. Her little belly is like velvet. There, take that—".

Here followed a desperate thrust.

"Oh!" from Julia.

Presently, a fantasy seized the salacious giant to gratify another lecherous idea, and carefully drawing his smoking member out of little Julia's tight parts he pushed himself between Bella's legs, and lodged it in her delicious slit. Up her young cunt went the big throbbing thing, while the owner slobbered out the ecstacy his exercise was giving him.

Julia looked on with amazement at the apparent ease with which the Father thrust his huge prick up into the white body of her friend.

After a quarter of an hour spent in this amatory position, during which Bella twice hugged the Father to her breast and emitted her warm tribute upon the head of his enormous yard, Clement once more withdrew, and sought to case himself of the hot spunk which was consuming him in the delicate person of the little Julia.

Taking that young lady in his arms, he once more threw himself upon her body, and, without much difficulty, pressing his burning prick upon her soft cunt, he prepared to deluge her interior with his wanton discharge.

A furious shower of deep and short pushes ensued, at the end of which Clement, with a loud sob, pressed deeply into the delicate girl, and commenced to pour a perfect deluge of semen into her. Jet after jet escaped from him, as, with upturned eyes and trembling limbs, the ecstasy seized upon him.

Julia's feelings were roused to the full, and she joined her ravisher in the final paroxysm with a degree of fierce rapture no flea can describe.

The orgies of that lascivious night are past my powers of description. No sooner had Clement recovered from his first libation, than in the grossest language he announced his intention of enjoying Bella, and immediately attacked her with his redoutable member.

For a full quarter of an hour he lay buried to the hairs in her belly, spinning out his enjoyment until Nature once more gave way, and Bella received his discharge in her womb.

Clement produced a cambric handkerchief, on which he wiped the streaming cunts of the two beauties. The two girls now took his member in their united grasp, and with tender and lascivious touches so excited the warm temperament of the Priest, that he stood again with a force and virility impossible to describe. His huge penis, made red and more swollen by his previous exercise, menaced the pair as they pawed it first in this direction and then in that. Several times Bella sucked the hot tip and tickled the open urethra with her pointed tongue.

This was evidently a favourite mode of enjoyment with Clement, and he quickly pushed as much of the big plum into the girl's mouth as he could insert.

Then he rolled them over and over, naked as they were born, glueing his fat lips to their reeking cunt in succession. He smacked and moulded their round buttocks, and even pushed his finger up their bottom-holes.

Then Clement and Bella between them persuaded Julia

to allow the Priest to insert the apex of his penis into her mouth, and after a considerable time spent in tickling and exciting the monstrous cock, he ejected such a torrent down the girl's throat and gullet that it nearly choked her.

A short interval ensued, and once more the unwonted enjoyment of two such tempting young and delicate girls roused Clement to his full vigour.

Placing them side by side he thrust his member alternately into each, and after a few fierce movements withdrew and entered the one unoccupied. Then he lay on his back, and drawing the girls upon him, sucked the cunt of one, while the other lowered herself upon his big prick, until their hairs met. Again and again he spouted into them his prolific essence.

The dawn alone put an end to the monstrous scene of debauchery.

But while such scenes as this were passing in the house, a very different one was rapidly approaching in the chamber of Mr. Verbouc, and when, three days afterwards, Ambrose returned from another absence, it was to find his friend and patron at the point of death.

A few hours sufficed to end the life and experiences of this eccentric gentleman.

After his decease, his window, never very intellectual, began to develop symptoms of insanity; in the paroxysm of which she perpetually called for the Priest, and when an aged and respectable Father had on one occasion been hastily summoned, the good lady indignantly denied that he could be an ecclesiastic, and demanded "the one with the big tool." Her language and behavior having scandalised all, she was incarcerated in an asylum, and there continued her ravings for the big prick.

Bella, thus left without protectors, readily lent ear to the solicitations of her Confessor, and consented to take the veil.

Julia, also an orphan, determined to share her friend's fate, and her mother's consent being readily given, both young ladies were received into the arms of Holy Mother Church upon the same day, and when the noviciate was past, both accordingly took the vows and the veil.

How those vows of chastity were kept, it is not for me, a humble flea, to dilate upon. I only know that after the ceremony was over, both girls were privately conveyed to the seminary, where some fourteen Priests awaited them.

Hardly allowing the new devotees the necessary time to divest themselves of their clothing, the wretches, furious at the prospect of so rich a treat, rushed upon them, and one by one satisfied their devilish lust.

Bella received upwards of twenty fervent discharges in every conceivable fashion; and Julia, hardly less vigorously assailed, at length fainted under the exhaustion caused by the rough treatment she experienced.

The chamber was well secured, no interruption was to be feared, and the sensual Brotherhood, assembled to do honour to the recently admitted sisters, revelled in their enjoyment to their heart's content.

Ambrose was there, for he had long seen the impossibility of attempting to keep Bella to himself, and, moreover, feared the animosity of his "confreres."

Clement was of the party, and his enormous member made havoc of the young charms he attacked.

The superior also had now the opportunity of indulging his antiphysical tastes; and not even the recently deflowered and delicate Julia escaped the ordeal of his assault. She had to submit, and with indescribable and hideous emotions of pleasure, he showered his viscid semen into her bowel.

The cries of those who discharged, the hard breathing of those labouring in the sensual act, the shaking and the groaning of the furniture, the half-uttered, half-suppressed conversation of the lookers on, all tended to magnify the libididinous monstrousity of the scene, and to deepen and render yet more revolting the details of this ecclesiastic pandemonium.

Oppressed with these ideas, and disgusted beyond measure at the orgie, I fled. I never stopped until I had put some miles between myself and the actors in the hateful drama, nor have I since cared to renew my familiarity with either Bella or Julia.

That they became the ordinary means of sensual gratification to the immates of the seminaty, I know. No doubt the constant and vigorous sensual excitement they endured, tended very soon to break up those beautiful young harms which had so worked upon me. Be that as it may; my task is done, my promise is performed, my memoir is ended, and if it is out of the power of a Flea to point a moral, at least it is not beyond his ability to choose his own pastures. Having had quite enough of those of which I have discoursed, I did as many are doing, who, although not Fleas, are, nevertheless as I reminded my readers in the commencement of my narrative, Bloodsuckers;—I emigrated.

THE END

MORE EROTIC CLASSICS FROM CARROLL & GRAF

☐ Anonymous/AUTOBIOGRAPHY OF A FLEA	$3.95
☐ Anonymous/CELEBRATED MISTRESS	$3.95
☐ Anonymous/DANGEROUS AFFAIRS	$3.95
☐ Anonymous/THE EDUCATION OF A MAIDEN	$3.95
☐ Anonymous/THE EROTIC READER	$3.95
☐ Anonymous/THE EROTIC READER II	$3.95
☐ Anonymous/MADELEINE	$3.95
☐ Anonymous/MAID'S NIGHT IN	$3.95
☐ Anonymous/THE MEMOIRS OF JOSEPHINE	$3.95
☐ Anonymous/MICHELE	$3.95
☐ Anonymous/CONFESSIONS OF EVELINE	$3.95
☐ Anonymous/VENUS IN INDIA	$3.95
☐ Anonymous/VENUS DISPOSES	$3.95
☐ Anonymous/VENUS REMEMBERED	$3.95
☐ Anonymous/VENUS UNMASKED	$3.95
☐ Anonymous/VICTORIAN FANCIES	$3.95
☐ van Heller, Marcus/THE LIONS OF AMON	$3.95
☐ Von Falkensee, Margarete/BLUE ANGEL NIGHTS	$3.95

Available from fine bookstores everywhere or use this coupon for ordering:

Caroll & Graf Publishers, Inc., 260 Fifth Avenue, N.Y., N.Y. 10001

Please send me the books I have checked above. I am enclosing $_____ (please add $1.75 per title to cover postage and handling.) Send check or money order—no cash or C.O.D.'s please. N.Y. residents please add 8¼% sales tax.

Mr/Mrs/Miss _____

Address _____

City _____ State/Zip _____

Please allow four to six weeks for delivery.
